PRAISE FOR NICOLE GIVENS KURTZ

"Nicole Givens Kurtz's The Spirit Room has William Faulkner rolling in his grave — and that's exactly what Southern Gothic needs. With a keen eye to character and place, this collection gives a needed voice to the people and stories America looks past. Beautiful and haunting."

ELIZABETH BROADBENT, AUTHOR OF *INK VINE* AND *BLOOD CYPRESS*

"Powerful, profound, and gut-wrenching, each story within *The Spirit Room* cuts deep on an emotional level. Kurtz confronts the harsh reality of urban America in vivid detail with bullet-like precision. These words will leave scars on your soul and tears in your eyes."

CANDACE NOLA, AUTHOR OF *SHADOW MANOR*

"Exposing the terror of both the seen and the unseen, *The Spirit Room* is at once titillating, galvanizing, and alarmingly keen. This is Southern Gothic Horror fully realized."

L. MARIE WOOD, BRAM STOKER AWARD® WINNER AND AUTHOR OF *THE RED THREAD SAGA*

"Brilliant Southern Gothic stories exploring both supernatural and human horrors through compelling characters."

THE SPIRIT ROOM

NICOLE GIVENS KURTZ

FIRST PUBLICATION ACKNOWLEDGEMENTS AND AWARD INFORMATION

The following works were first published in these anthologies and magazines, or performed on these podcasts, with much gratitude from the author:

"Speechless" was first published in *Under Her Eye: A Women in Horror Poetry Showcase, Volume II* (2023, Black Spot Books)

"Sweet Tooth" was first published in *The Big Bad II* (2015, Dark Oak Press)

"Dogwood Stories" debuted in *Diabolical Plots* (2019, May issue)

"The Guardian" won a 2021 Atomacon Palmetto Scribe Award for Best Short Story, and was first published in *Twenty-two Speculative Stories by Black Women Writers* (2020, Midnight & Indigo)

"As Dark the Night" was first featured in *Hybrids: Misfits, Monsters, and Other Phenomena* (2022, Hybrid Sequence Media)

"The Tell-Tale Tattoo" was initially published in *Nevermore: An Anthology Inspired by Edgar Alan Poe* (2024, Fallstaff Books)

"Lipstick Smile" debuted on *Nightlight: A Horror Fiction Podcast* (Season 1, Episode 16, Ransom Media Productions)

"Sunshine" was first published in *Black Girl Magic Magazine* (2016, July issue)

FIRST PUBLICATION ACKNOWLEDGEMENTS AND AWARD INFORMATION

"Dark August Rain" was first published in *Rain* (2016, Horrified Press)

SOUTHERN GOTHIC
– A DEFINITION

According to Oxford Research Literature:

Southern Gothic is a mode or genre prevalent in literature from the early 19th century to this day. Characteristics of Southern Gothic include the presence of irrational, horrific, and transgressive thoughts, desires, and impulses; grotesque characters; dark humor, and an overall angst-ridden sense of alienation. While related to both the English and American Gothic tradition, Southern Gothic is uniquely rooted in the South's tensions and aberrations. During the 20th century, Charles Crow has noted, the South became "the principal region of American Gothic" in literature. The Southern Gothic brings to light the extent to which the idyllic vision of the pastoral, agrarian South rests on massive repressions of the region's historical realities: slavery, racism, and patriarchy. Southern Gothic texts also mark a Freudian return of the repressed: the region's historical realities take concrete forms in the shape of ghosts that highlight all that has been unsaid in the official version of southern history (Bjerre, 2017).

THE
SPIRIT
ROOM

SPEECHLESS

My voice grinds on the ears,
on the fragile and weak,
with their long vowels and clipped ends.

My voice crunches on those egos,
and punctures the blown-up and puffy privilege
and swollen bags of pride.

Yet, they remain.
Like ivory kudzu spreading and sprawling.
Blanketing my output, stimming my growth,
choking me to silence.

My hands are scraped and scarred
from clearing out
my throat.

SWEET TOOTH

ryce Howerton disliked black licorice. It tasted like leftover ash mixed with high fructose corn syrup—something burnt and overly sweetened. After spitting it out, he couldn't get the aftertaste to fade. There just wasn't enough bubblegum to mask the lingering coat on his tongue. He scratched his itchy cornrow braids and spat again. It seemed to be glazed all over his mouth, and he continued to rake his tongue over his teeth in an attempt to clear it. Walking along the cracked and broken sidewalk that threaded through weathered brick apartments, Bryce and Marquis were killing time on a lazy, fall afternoon.

"I just bought that," complained Marquis between wet, loud licks of his cherry lollipop. His eyes followed the hunk of black-licorice-colored spittle. "I coulda used that dollar for a pop."

Bryce shrugged. He dug around his threadbare jeans pockets, and his heart brightened when his fingers brushed another crinkled dollar. Hmph. That was for *his* pop. With his other hand, he held up the remaining offensive licorice. "Nasty."

But *nasty* didn't cover it. Bryce frowned at the twisted waxy piece of candy leftover in his fist. Marquis didn't get it. Anything coming out of Momma Shug's place couldn't be trusted. Why he hadn't told Bryce where he bought it until *after* he'd put it in his mouth bothered him. A brother deserved fair warning.

"You should've told me where you got it."

"Why that matter?" Marquis asked idly. Most of his concentration centered on the collection of change in his open palm. His lips moved as he counted how much money he had left.

Bryce opened his mouth to answer, but shut it firm. He couldn't explain it to Marquis, or anyone. Most people didn't notice the strangeness around Momma Shug's place. Bryce had been watching her his whole life. Now, at thirteen, he couldn't remember a time when neighborhood peeps didn't buy sugar delights from her or a time when the police didn't find random bodies all around the projects, scattered and hidden in the brush and garbage piles like morbid Easter eggs. Hood life was so sour, so full of lemons, your lips, heck your *soul*, puckered. Anything sweet would do to give some pleasure. Hell, babies came out, full dark lips in a round o, seeking refuge from the bitter taste of hopelessness solidified by 39 weeks of stress in an angst-filled womb.

Was it any wonder kids flocked to Momma Shug's?

He glanced at Marquis. A brother deserved fair warning, didn't he?

Because of the bodies. These weren't like the kills of gangbangers. No, no. The corpses Bryce and his friends found had withered opened eyes, mouths frozen in terrified screams and fear. All the bodies looked like they'd been sucked dry of all living goodness.

They don't do nuthin' for the Black and the missing.

Bryce's neighbor always said: No one care about a bunch of poor Black young'un gone missing.

One time, she'd asked him. "How come *you* always findin' 'em bodies?"

Bryce looked her dead in the eyes. "'Cause nobody care about the Black and the missin'."

She smiled then—a sad one.

He couldn't tell her either, about Momma Shug.

Bryce adjusted his jeans and tried to spit far away from his Carolina hoodie. Nothing as freakin' gross as this licorice should touch his Carolina blue. Marquis wore a Carolina jersey, too, but underneath, he wore a white t-shirt. They'd both gotten their hair braided and new clothes in anticipation of the local block party. A cold breeze rushed by and moved Bryce's earring, a tiny gold hoop. Most boys had what looked like diamond studs, but he hated the cubic zirconium. It didn't seem real. The last thing he wanted was an infected ear the size of a doughnut. Besides, he could think of other things to spend his money on.

Marquis started busting rhymes to fill in the awkward silence between them. Every once in a while, Bryce would toss in a "yeah" to keep the flow going, but his heart wasn't in it.

Nor his mind. They passed the rec center playground. Dirt-smeared yellow caution tape flapped in the wind. Last week, they'd found a body. Another body. Bryce had seen it, tossed along the cluster of rusty dumpsters, wedged between the stained, filthy mattresses someone had thrown out. Someone had tossed out a human being, along with so much trash. It reeked of rotting flesh and old garbage. Bryce knew it—*her,* Cynthia. He'd seen her getting her goodies at

Momma Shug's just a few hours before finding her behind the dumpster. It had been him who went searching for her and called in the "anonymous" tip. He'd hung up before the 911 lady could ask his name. Bryce didn't have a death wish. Snitches got stitches.

But Cyndi deserved to be found, and soon, before her baby cousin came down to play ball at the rec. Cyndi had been his friend throughout all of elementary—not his good friend. The girl ate too many sweets and stole from his trick-or-treat bag, but she didn't deserve that kinda death.

Candy wraps had been tossed across her chest like she'd been some sort of treat.

Goosebumps spread over Bryce's arms at the memory. He hunched back into his hoodie, seeking warmth. He shot a quick glance at Marquis. With his memory of the discovery still in pieces, he felt his warm blood trickle down his chin.

"Dang bruh! You bleedin'!" Marquis pointed out with his pinky, the fingernail long and yellowing.

Using the back of his hand, Bryce wiped it away. It didn't matter how much he swiped, he couldn't get the taste out of his mouth. The candy sank like a stone into a lake, falling deeper and deeper into his core. His stomach churned at the impact. The scent of burned *something* clung to his nose, pushed its odor into his brain, and with each intake of breath came the scent.

He coughed hard to dislodge the odor. Red brick dust crunched like grit in his mouth.

"You bite your tongue or something?" Marquis pointed at him with the lollipop.

"No, I, I think this stupid licorice poked my cheek. It ain't no big deal," Bryce tried to sound brave, tried to make

Marquis think he didn't care about the blood the licorice caused. Now he had ash, sugar, and copper flavors in his mouth, and a swelling in his throat.

"Dang! It tastes like crap."

"How come you know what crap tastes like?" Marquis countered, smirking broadly. He licked his candy again, slurping the scarlet treat between his full lips. When he caught Bryce's frown, he laughed.

"Shut up." Bryce pretended to kick a rock.

They had walked up the hill from the rec center, having shot a few rounds of ball before deciding to eat the treats Marquis had bought from Momma Shug's. Now with the rec and the hill at their backs, they approached the government-produced apartments. Each one bled into its neighbor, becoming a smear of identical front doors and concrete porches. The housing projects didn't do much in way of décor or distinction—cheap housing for the poor didn't warrant any type of luxury.

Bryce had been born and raised in Holmes Housing Projects, but he knew that off of Rose Street, the third apartment from the curb always looked dark. Bright sunny summer days still found the porch somber and gloomy. Shadows huddled there en masse, defying the sun's bright cheeriness. It didn't matter how much light was out, didn't matter about the streetlights neither, the doorway of that apartment—Momma Shug's—held darkness—like she collected it or something. All huddled up against the concrete porch and cheap siding.

"You wanna go trade for that bad candy?" Marquis asked. "She'll let you git somethin' else."

The hairs on the back of Bryce's neck stood up.

Momma Shug's hollowed cheeks and wrinkling skin appeared in his mind like a specter. Her waxy skin shined like melted chocolate on the hot asphalt in the summer. Round, red-rimmed eyes peered out from beneath the fall of thick silver braids, matted with beads and ribbons and *life*. She smelled of death and sweetness—not all that different from his licorice. No, he didn't want any more of Momma Shug's candy.

"Nah, I'm good."

He wasn't, but he wouldn't let Marquis know. A man had to keep his pride. No way would he let Marquis know how freaking scared he was of that woman. Bryce took two more steps. When he realized Marquis wasn't in step with him, he turned back around with dread piling into his already uneasy belly.

Marquis put the entire sucker in his mouth once more. Even from this distance, Bryce could see a single sliver of drool roll down the corner of his mouth. Marquis didn't move, didn't blink, and didn't breathe.

"Come on, man, snap out of it." Bryce gently shook him. The cold wash of fear slipped across his shoulders. "Wipe that off your chin."

"Huh?"

The rattling of metal against the broken sidewalk's asphalt coupled with the bubbling of rubber wheels and the clanging of metal set Bryce's teeth on edge. He glanced up just in time to see Momma Shug, hunched over and bent, pushing a stolen shopping cart. Like most shopping carts, the right wheel wobbled over the cracked sidewalk. Cardboard boxes brimmed with colorful wrapped candy sat in the spot where a child would go. Her candy cart sliced through the chilly afternoon. Each step she took carried the promise of her sugary treats.

And death. Bryce swallowed the hard knot of acid-mixed fear and ash. *What the hell did she put in that licorice?*

At the sound of her cart, Marquis came to life. "There she is! You can swap it out now! Tell her it was nasty."

"Uh, nah. I'm good."

Marquis gave him a hard look and then frowned.

"You ain't scared?"

"No," Bryce said with more bravery than he felt. He didn't want to be on Momma Shug's bad side. No one else would suspect it, but his instincts told him she had something to do with Cyndi's death. Like when he knew a drive-by was about to happen, or when he knew to stay in his room when his foster momma's boyfriend came over to visit. No one told him; he just *knew.*

"Yeah, you are!" Marquis laughed, but it sliced short. It melded into a gaggle, a choking cough.

"Man, what's your..."

Bryce dropped his sour taffy to the ground and watched in horror as Marquis's face grayed. Choking! Adrenaline burst through Bryce and he got behind Marquis. He couldn't remember how to do that thing he was supposed to do, but he did know to take both his hands, clasp them together, and put them under the ribs. He pumped. A wheezing rattle came from Marquis's mouth, but not the chunk of ruby candy lodged in his airway.

"Come on!" Bryce used all of his strength, prayed and cried as he tried to help clear his friend's airway. "Man, don't do this!"

Marquis's chest rattled when his mouth opened. The air

whistled around the sphere in his throat. The sickening sound fueled Bryce's determination. He squinted over Marquis's shoulder to Momma Shug. An open-mouth grin took up most of her face. Those coal-black eyes seemed to gleam in joy. Bryce couldn't look away from those dark pits. Darkness poured out, glistening tar-sticky thick and inescapable. He heard nothing but the rasp of Marquis's labored attempts to breathe.

The trembling and rising panic made Marquis contort and flail his body. All made it that much harder to hold him still.

"Stop moving! Dude! I'm trying to help."

Marquis gave some primal gurgle, mixed with sorrow. It was the most terrifying sound Bryce had ever heard.

"Help!" The suddenly vacant street struck Bryce as strange. On most days, the yards, street corners, and flat porches crawled with people, just hanging out, throwing dice or doing hair, just shooting the breeze.

He realized then the bustle of project life, the rise and fall of bass-booming music thumping from passing cars, the guffaws from foolishness and corner-store beer, and the sharp shouting of disagreements that were all there before, like a living, breathing chorus, were gone. He scanned the neighborhood. Nothing moved. No sound. It didn't feel right, not normal. For one, this was Saturday. Clear skies. First of the month. They'd disappeared the moment Momma Shug appeared.

"Stop doing it!" he yelled across the still air.

"Stop what?" She sounded like a thousand voices mashed and then flattened. He'd never get that voice out of his head.

"This! We need help!" Tears huddled at the corners of his eyes. He gripped Marquis closer to him and heaved, his hands acting now on instinct.

"Would you like a sweet? You need a sweet!" She stretched out her withered hand toward him. Three eyeballs, whole with the optic nerve still attached, pooled in the middle of her palm.

Bryce scrambled backward, taking Marquis with him. "Stop it!"

She merely smiled at him—her empty mouth like a cave.

Not today. Nobody else gonna die.

He resumed the maneuver, shoving his panic deep while his anger rose. She wasn't taking any more of his friends. Cyndi would be the last. The day inched on, and Bryce lost track of time. Only two minutes went by, but it could've been two years.

Momma Shug stopped a few feet away.

Instead of lending a hand, she rubbed hers together, like she was ready for a feast.

She looks hungry.

"Come on, dude," Bryce partially prayed and whispered aloud.

He heaved again, before a hacking *splat* hit the sidewalk. Bright, scarlet and still whole, the salvia-drenched hunk of candy cracked on the sidewalk in a watery pink pool. Marquis screamed, stumbled out of Bryce's arms, and collapsed in a heap to the sidewalk. Rubbing his throat, he tried to stand.

"You alright?" Bryce held his elbow as he stood up.

"Yeah," Marquis croaked out. His face furrowed in pain.

Suddenly, he hunched over; Bryce grabbed him again. Something was wrong. "Momma..."

She—*it*—cackled. A sound from behind him caught his attention, but when he turned back to Momma Shug, she was gone. Only the shopping cart remained. Its busted wheel creaking in the cold breeze.

Marquis slacked back into Bryce's arms. The rise and fall of his skinny chest heaved once more.

Only once.

⸺

Four days later

"It isn't your fault, baby. You did whatcha could." Marquis's momma hugged Bryce before releasing him.

He shuffled through the procession of mourners outside the Fourth Street Baptist Church. Words were said. Songs, somber and serious, were sung. Numbness hung over him, so none of it penetrated. Well, that wasn't all true. The persistent hot burn of fury kept him up and refused to wink out. Two days ago, he realized that he couldn't cry. This level of pissed-off torched all his grief—only white-hot heat of revenge remained.

He walked back home, and he found his older foster brother, Tre, sitting on the front porch they shared with the neighbors.

"Aye, you heard. Shit around here is cray-cray."

Bryce sat. Just after one on Wednesday, peeps slept in because they just *got* in. Others were at church. So, he and

Tre held down the front yard. Rain poured into already flooded corners of the lawns and backed up sewers. Bryce touched his cheek and winced. The injury from the licorice still hurt. He spat out pink spittle onto the sidewalk again.

"Yeah."

Tre smoked a black and mild cigarette. "They ain't seen Tasha since yesterday."

"Damn."

"Yeah. Her momma called the cops. They said she a runaway."

Bryce hunched back into his hoodie. Nowadays he was cold, always cold. "That's what they always say 'bout us."

"True dat." Tre blew a stream of sweet-smelling smoke.

"We runaways or dealin'. Our deaths don't matter."

"'Cept to us."

Bryce shoved his fists into his hoodie's pockets. Tre didn't have it wrong. Cops didn't give a shit about this neighborhood, not that it mattered. They couldn't stop Momma Shug, anyway.

"Yeah. 'Cept to us," Bryce muttered, a grin inching across his face.

"We handle our own ish."

Bryce stood up. "Yeah. We do."

THE NINE-MILLIMETER HANDGUN FELT STRANGE IN Bryce's hand. He'd climbed the concrete stairs to his room and shut the door. No curtains, so the day's full gloominess poured in. He had found Tre on his bed watching the day travel on, a paper bag in his lap.

"You sure you know what you doin'?" Tre now stood by Bryce's bedroom window. "Thought you didn't want in the gang."

"I don't." Bryce shoved the gun into his backpack. Along the floor, his now expelled textbooks sat next to his sneakers.

"So whatcha need that piece for?" Tre didn't turn to look at him.

"'Cause the world is cray-cray." Bryce heard the harshness in his tone.

Tre flinched, then smirked. "Well, damn."

"Sorry."

Tre faced him. "I know you got a lot goin' on since 'Quis died. I don't need to know whatcha doin'. You one of the smartest peeps I know, so you probably know whatcha doin'. That's good enough for me."

With that, Tre left.

Bryce took up the spot at his window and waited for nightfall. "I hope so."

* * *

Later that evening

A FAT MOON, FULL OF LIGHT, RESTED ON THICK clouds overhead. Bryce walked quickly to his destination. Porch lights acted as guides, illuminating his course. Sweaty palms, quivering stomach, and the cold handgun's metal biting into the small of his back made him uneasy. His hoodie covered it from others' views, but he knew it was there. Each step served to remind him.

Too soon, he reached his destination and knocked on the door. The inside of his cheek burned and filled his mouth with the taste of ash and blood.

Before he could spit, the door creaked open. "Yes?"

"I wanna buy some candy." He coughed over the lie.

Momma Shug, wearing a thread-bare sweater, broom skirt and slippers, grinned. Her black hair-wrap made it look like she only had eyes, nose, and a mouth. Through thick glasses, she peered at him.

"I know you."

Bryce shuddered.

"I have just what you want." She receded into the apartment's dark.

Bryce reached behind him, put his hand on his gun, and followed her inside.

The place smelled just as it had before—sweetness and dirt. Like it had been closed up and not aired out for decades. Bryce tried to hold his breath. She led him through the dim living room and to the back room—the kitchen. There an orange light cast shadows on the wall. On a table sat several boxes of candy clearly labeled with prices. She turned to him.

"Here."

Bryce peered at her. Small. Frail. Hunched over, bent by time and age, Momma Shug didn't seem threatening. He released the gun and put both hands in his hoodie's pockets. His cheek throbbed and his mouth felt full of warm blood.

"This isn't what you want, is it?" Momma Shug asked, removing her glasses. "Be honest. You aren't here for these kind of sweets..."

"No, no ma'am, I'm not. I thought..." He stopped. What did he think?

She stood up to her full height, the hunch vanishing before his eyes. Bryce stumbled backward, his hands failing to grab the gun.

"What the hell are you?"

Momma Shug grinned, and this time her mouth held nice, neat rows of teeth. "You really don't know, do you?"

"Know what?" Bryce's hand shook as his hand found the gun at last. He pulled it from its hiding spot and felt the calm of power steady him. "Huh? Know what? That you killed all them kids? Sucking out souls like some demon."

Momma Shug laughed. A thousand voices flattened into one. "I didn't kill anyone."

"Liar!" Bryce squeezed the trigger.

Firing this close to Momma Shug should've dropped her like a sack of potatoes. Instead, she flickered like a faulty light switch and became solid once more. She peered at him with eyes now clear and free of cataracts.

"Between feedings, you tend to forget. You love the sugar high, but the crash makes you blank out. This is one of your worst, though. Marquis wasn't sweet enough, was he?"

Bryce shut his eyes. "What? No, no..."

"Yes, *son*..."

Son. Son? The gun shook in his fist, then fell to the floor. Memory flashes sliced with sharp, stinging precision. The kiss he and Cyndi shared out behind the rec center. Her screams. Her blood siphoned like a Slurpee. All consumed until only the husk remained. Bryce's hand scattering crinkled wrappers across the body. The visions blurred. Then rail-thin Marquis fell into his arms. Bryce's feeding tubular stabbed Marquis's ear. Gut-wrenching gurgling as Bryce took huge sips of his life. The delight he took in consuming their sugar-drenched blood wrecked through him.

Bryce fell to his knees. "No. It—it's a trick. A mind trick!"

At that moment, the burning in his cheek flared. Something else moved in his mouth, and it wasn't his tongue. Screaming, Bryce opened his mouth and out shot a flesh-toned tubular. It searched the air, seeking sweetness, hungry. Momma Shug wasn't hungry. He was! Holding his hand over his cheek, Bryce shuddered as the cold realization filtered over him.

Him.

It had been him all along. Tears fell to the floor.

"You lying!" he roared around the tubular. "LIAR!"

Momma Shug opened the pantry's door and inside was a bound and gagged Tasha. She wiggled and thrashed. Not traditional food in this pantry, but a living and breathing girl.

"You brought her over right after the funeral..." Momma Shug fingered one of the girl's curls.

"No!" Bryce shut his eyes tight to banish the nightmare. Tasha's muffled whimpering broke through and wrenched him mentally back into the room. Had it all been true? His head hurt and he staggered to his feet. The long appendage hanging out of his mouth spoke to the truth. It was real. Gooey and seeking substance. That hadn't been a trick.

Tasha's eyes widened when she saw him, but not in relief —in fear.

At this, his memory block broke and out poured truth. Momma Shug squeezing his hand. Scores of countless faces filled his vision. Scoops of flesh. Hunks of humans. Greedily consumed, happily munched—by him. He'd witnessed decades dawn and set. No teenager, but infinite, posing as a foster kid in the projects to fit in. To feed easier. Always coming back to his real mother when he needed to—when he needed *her*. Bryce looked up at Momma Shug. She fed the stock candy to sweeten their blood, so when they fed, it was delicious—marinating the meat. All those faces and countless surprised expressions frozen in time. Those sweet treats they scarfed down made them tasty—er. Little flesh cakes filled with delicious, dark red filling. He reeled in his tubular, now on reflex, as his true nature returned.

"You remember." It wasn't a question. She stepped back from Tasha. "You must've come home seeking something sweet."

Bryce nodded. "Thanks, Momma."

Momma Shug came to stand beside him. With her hot breath on his cheek, she patted his shoulder. "You always had one hell of a sweet tooth."

"Late bloomers have the prettiest blooms," Sadie's momma said after she tapped her on the head with the comb. "So, stop squirmin'."

"It's too tight." Sadie winced, sucking in air to offset the pain. Her scalp burned like someone had set fire to it. She put her hands in her lap and tried to weather the storm, her hands rubbing each other to soothe the pain.

"Tenderheaded. That's all." Her momma pinched off a section of hair and began another braid.

Sadie stifled a groan and squeezed her eyes tight. Once her momma finished the braid, she rubbed a finger full of grease along the parts, oiling her scalp and providing a balm to her irritated skin. The braids still hurt, the hair pulled taut and confined in the creative style.

With her hands sweating, Sadie gritted her teeth and stopped complaining. Not cause her momma's braiding had stopped hurting. It did, but she wanted to look nice for the Dogwood Arts Festival. It happened once a year in Knoxville and she loved the early spring weather. Fresh grass, the flowers' sweet smells, and the pollen giving everything a yellow hue.

Here in East Tennessee, beneath the Great Smoky Mountains' rolling hills and purple peaks, the dogwood reigned. The annual festival honoring dogwood trees and their lore of bestowing blessings included barbeques and reminiscing about history. Heck, there was even bacon. Knoxville lay at the foot of the Smokies, in the valley. Protected to the east by mountains and blessed by the Tennessee River flowing through it, the city of Knoxville bloomed after the 1982 World's Fair. Sadie only heard stories. The impact on the small county—caused the town to morph into a metropolis.

"Momma?"

"Yeah, baby?" Her momma popped her gum. The rush of spearmint tickled Sadie's nose. Her hands rested heavy against Sadie's head.

"Tell me about the dogwoods." Sadie opened her eyes and waited. She loved when her momma read or told her stories about their people. The truth and all its messy bits her teachers didn't tell her about in school. That's what her momma called it—messy bits.

Momma's stories went back as far as the Dogwood Arts Festival itself. Some of the stories Momma got from Grand-momma, Sadie's Nana. Knoxville didn't have a lot of folks who looked like her. Most of Sadie's schooling had been by middle-class white women, some well meaning, but confined by stereotypical beliefs and hatred, both festering inside and foaming outside in whitewashed facts. So, when her momma talked about history, their history, in her rich, southern drawl, Sadie would disappear into those words melting into the past. Those logs fueled her inner fire to burn through the present's challenges.

"Well, back in the days, a long time ago, the dogwood was strong, as strong as the oak tree. The people who kilt

Jesus used the dogwood to make the crosses people was crucified on. The dogwood was a killin' tree. So when they kilt Jesus on the cross, God twisted the dogwood, punished it by making its limbs thin and skinny..."

"So no one could be crucified on them anymore," Sadie finished, her heart hammering in glee.

"Right. But just so folk don't forget, God made the white petals of the dogwood look like a cross, four points, with blood bracketed on the tips where they put the nails in Jesus." Her momma breathed deep and sad as she started braiding again. "Dunno why you like that story so much. It's sad, Sadie."

"It isn't sad, Momma. It's beautiful." Sadie sat up straighter against the couch.

"You a strange child." Her momma tapped her shoulder. "You done."

Sadie stood. Her legs ached from sitting, but the searing of her scalp blotted that out. Still, she took the stairs two at a time to get changed. Soon, her cousin, Tina, would be by and together they'd make their way downtown to the festival.

She changed clothes from her pajama bottoms and t-shirt into jeans and a long-sleeved, white University of Tennessee t-shirt. The words *Go Big Orange* spelled out in vibrant U.T. orange. Sadie thought about the dogwoods. She loved the story, not because of God's punishment of the dogwood. The trees had been changed. Their strength had been used for evil, to hurt people, to inflict suffering. Unable to stop the people from using them for this purpose, the dogwood had been relieved of the burden. She didn't see it as a punishment, so much as the dogwood being freed.

No, the dogwoods did not belong to white Jesus or his believers. The dogwood belonged to Black folks—southern Black folks. Like the dogwood, they'd suffered, blooms of potential sliced off by hatred vile and black as the skin of those they despised. Such "nice folks" capable of such monstrous acts as decorating beautiful grand oak and magnolia trees with bodies as ornaments. Smiling families lined up to take pictures in front of those macabre Christmas trees. Those dark, empty husks, dusty and lifeless, had been her family, her people, her kin.

Sadie sat down on the edge of her bed. Not the dogwood. Its petals already bore the bloodstain of death. Mostly, the thick oaks and redwoods found themselves defined by evil.

The faint knocks announced Tina's arrival.

Sadie slapped on her gold bangle bracelets and her big gold hoop earrings.

"You comin', Sadie?" her momma shouted up the stairs to her. "Tina's down here waitin'."

Sadie checked her braids in the mirror. Her hoops glistened along with the glossy and thick braids. Her head ached a little, but the rising excitement flooded her with a glow that numbed the pain.

"Yeah. Ready." She scooped up her pocketbook and headed downstairs.

Once Sadie reached the bottom of the stairs, she found Tina and her momma in the living room. The front door stood ajar, but the screen door remained open. Outside, the lemon-yellow sun beamed in the early afternoon sky. Sadie rounded the short corner and walked into the living room—and a debate.

"That's so 80s. We done did that." Her momma stood with her arms akimbo on her wide hips, watching Tina. Her satin, multi-colored headwrap hid most of her hair, except her tight spiral curls around her face. She wore a loose blue dress with pockets and house shoes she wore outside.

Her cousin's box braids swung about her flared hips as she rotated in a circle, shaking her hip-hugging and strategically ripped jeans. Sadie's momma laughed, throwing back her head, mouth wide, and humor crinkling the corners of her eyes.

Sadie shrugged. "Everything dies. But then it comes back."

The chuckles stopped. Tina turned to peer at Sadie, her forehead wrinkled in confusion.

"You such a weird child." Sadie's mom shook her head and, with scrunched eyebrows, turned back to straightening the living room. The smile left and shadows formed on her momma's face.

Remnants of the shed hair, combs, and decorative beads littered the couch and rug where Sadie had sat.

Sadie let the words glide off of her. Those labels, *strange* and *weird*, had become worn and faded to her ears. Blunted like a knife that had been used too much.

"It's a cycle, like spring. Renewal ..." Sadie explained to the back of her momma's head.

Tina rolled her eyes. "You got your pocketbook?" Her voice dipped so low only Sadie could hear. "Sassy Sadie, let's go."

"Bye, Momma." Sadie waved goodbye. The screen door slammed with a *whap*.

Once they got to Tina's little Honda Civic, she gave

Sadie the once-over. "Your braids are poppin'! Dang. They tight!"

"Yeah. Momma just finished them." Sadie shoved her hands into her jeans pockets. Eager to go, she fought to keep her hands busy while Tina fished her car keys out of her pocketbook. The silence filled her with dread. Energy buzzed across her skin like lightning, like Saturday morning on Volunteer Football gamedays.

Her cousin, Tina, lived up the street in a house that lined the edge of the projects' apartment buildings. Older by four years, Tina had her driver's license and an interest in art. The Dogwood Arts Festival local art show hosted a high school arts competition. Once the works were judged, students won ribbons and prizes. Tina had a few pieces showing, and she wanted to show them off to Sadie. That fact alone took sheer courage. Strength. Tina had blossomed from the poor, clay dirt into a creative flower.

"Ready?" Tina unlocked the car, climbed in, and started the ignition.

"Yeah!" Sadie said with relief. At last!

It seemed to take forever, but in no time, they'd made their way from Cherry Street to downtown Market Street. As Tina parked the car, Sadie rushed out of the passenger side before Tina could remove the key from the ignition. The air felt different. It spoke to her.

"Hold 'em horses, Sadie!" Tina called.

Sadie paused on the sidewalk. "Hurry up!"

Once she cleared the car, Tina tossed her braids. "I'm coming."

They melded with the crowds of people streaming toward Market Square, a sea of pale faces with occasional spots of color. The Dogwood Arts Festival's banners of white, mint green, and pink announced the celebration, but the trees showed off. Reaching high to the sky in all their splendor, they decorated Gay Street, the primary artery into Knoxville's heart—downtown.

Sadie took in the rows of glorious trees. The tension level swelled. People bumped and jostled as they took in the new blooms, the artists, and vendors selling all manner of items. Southern-fried foods' strong aromas wafted through the air. Pink, green, and white balloons decorated vendor and artisans' tables and booths along Market Square. The free event swelled with individuals beneath the cornflower-blue sky and the occasional white cotton-ball clouds.

Postcard perfect.

Sadie's Nana used to say firm footing could turn to quicksand in a blink.

Whispers circulated, like snakes slithering between people, hissing in warning, a pop, like firecrackers then a sharp burning sensation exploded in Sadie's chest. Her breath caught and a flash of bright light made her wince. She watched, transfixed, as a scarlet dot on her shirt blossomed across her heart, growing as if elapsed time had been fast-forwarded.

Sadie's joy gushed out with her blood. She couldn't feel anything except the soft, downy dogwood petals brushing her cheeks.

For a crowd of branches, they weren't shy about revealing themselves. Her face—hot and tight— couldn't move as the whispers intensified. The trees leaned down close to her, their branches cracking like dry spines, shifting to mutter their wisdom into her ears. Blood roared in her ears as adrenaline flooded her system. She gave a wheezing cough. As she removed her hand from her mouth, an awareness settled on her shoulders.

I've been shot.

Life ground to a halt.

Dogwoods didn't chase ghosts away. They were ghosts. Of her ancestors, of all ancestors of the strong and betrayed.

This. Was. It!

The moment the dogwoods welcomed her into their fold. All of Sadie's muscles strained as she lifted up her arms. They cradled her. The ivory petals stained with rust, by blood. Hers? Alarmed, she struggled, but their thin, rough bark tightened.

They whispered, "No matter. No matter. Only blood. We know it."

With this, they bobbed in the breeze and continued to convey their knowledge, such as the wonders of weather that affected their delicate branches and blooms, their wonderful stories of steam and coal, of feasts and famines, and of freedom.

"You been strong for so long," one dogwood said. It sounded like Nana.

"It hurts," Sadie croaked, mouth thick and lazy.

"Come on, chile. Rest awhile. Here..." said another dogwood tree.

"But..." Sadie said, "my momma..."

"...is gonna be alright, after a while," still another tree explained.

Their branches swayed as if cheering on this viewpoint.

"Hush. Hush," they soothed.

"Come. Come," they pleaded.

She savored every promise, every whispered word.

"I dunno…" Sadie started to turn away, to see the others in the marketplace. A coldness crept in, chilling her. She shuddered. A grisly, gruesome scene unfolded around her. "Tina."

"Come on, now. Do not be afraid." Nana's voice again. It sounded warm and syrupy with its Southern drawl, thick and sweet.

Sadie's eyelids grew heavy. Her throat burned, but she managed to say, "My momma, she needs me. I can't come with y'all now."

So hard to talk. Her tongue didn't want to work right. So tired.

Sadie closed her eyes among the dogwoods' sweet scent.

"This is Roberta Sneed with WBIR Channel 10 at the scene of what can only be described as a mass shooting. The incident happened shortly after three this afternoon at the Dogwood Arts Festival. Police are asking viewers to avoid the downtown area. The festival, usually a time for joy, spring, and renewal, now is a place of violence and death."

A few feet away, Tina shuddered beneath the blanket the EMS tossed over her shoulders. Yellow caution tape roped off the area as if it were some exclusive club that no one wanted to belong to—a survivor of a mass shooting. No one wanted the alternative either. Fate dealt her and Sadie a cruel blow. The reporter gave vague descriptions of the shooter. Tina scoffed. That cowardly bastard's soul was deformed.

The cops muttered about his deep-seated grudges, but Tina knew that evil took root in places folks don't always expect —and places they do.

The crime scene was a hive of activity. KPD and others dressed in POLICE jackets buzzed around the area, like flies among the corpses. A flurry of activity sped up and slowed down simultaneously. Was this shock?

"Blood everywhere." So bright against the white.

Tina's tears flowed so much her eyes swelled and burned. Noise. Wailing. Screams of sirens switched to soft humming and back again. Everything had become jumbled. Nothing made sense.

"Sadie?" she called out.

A short distance from where she stood, her little cousin, Sadie Griffin lay crumbled on the bricked plaza. She'd fallen where she stood. A duo of EMS folks hovered around her, blocking her view. Tina tried to distance herself from them as if she could melt into the blanket, a makeshift invisibility cloak.

Tina closed her eyes, stomach lurching. The scents of copper and gunpowder hung in the air, staining it with death. She couldn't even smell the dogwoods anymore.

Dogwoods.

Tina pictured Sadie's meddling with such freedom, but it had cost her. She could still see her, Sadie, practically bouncing in her excitement to be out at the festival. Now motionless. Struck down in her moment of joy.

Tina tasted the salt on her lips. She tasted pain. Grief. Of course, they were salty. Anger burned hot at the injustice of it. The police had caught the gunman—unharmed. That murderer would live.

Would her sweet cousin?

Tina remembered Sadie's face when the bullet plowed through her. Dogwood petals rained down on her. The wind blew them loose, but it looked like they wept at the ugliness of the day. Her dark, round eyes sparked as she watched the dogwoods sway in the breeze. Tina sighed and wiped her tears. She needed to be strong for her aunt and her family.

For Sadie.

"SHE'S AWAKE!" SADIE'S MOMMA'S SHOUT SEEMED to be piped in from far away. Despite this, the wavering thread of relief came through clear and defined. The thick scent of night-blooming jasmine hung along with the harsher hints of something else. Confused, Sadie's eyebrows knitted together. Too much light for it to be night. Sadie's everything hurt as she tried to move or sit up. She tried to open her eyes, but the lights hurt, too. But in that brief eyeful, she could tell she wasn't in her bedroom.

"Where am I?" she managed through cottonmouth. Her lips crackled, and she winced again. Each motion brought agony. So she tried to stay still.

"Here. Drink." Her momma handed her a cup of water.

She leaned up on one elbow. Sadie drank, but the I.V. pulled her dry skin on her hand. It bled.

"You at U.T. Hospital." Her momma rubbed her hair and took the cup.

Hospital?

Once her eyes adjusted to the glare and the fluorescent's

harshness, she looked around the room, as much as she could without moving too much. Then it all rushed back to the forefront of her mind. She'd been shot!

"Momma, the dogwoods!" Sadie said and struggled to sit up fully. The atmosphere shifted as if a certain emotion had been vanquished by her newfound secret knowledge. "The dogwoods are alive! More than that, they spoke."

Maybe Tina heard it too, Sadie thought.

"Shush, baby girl. They gonna be here. Just like e'ry year." Her momma kissed her forehead.

Suddenly exhausted, Sadie shut her eyes. Those dogwoods wagging their blooms all over town, running the thread about the foolishness of men. Tossing away life like ruined and withered petals.

Sadie knew it because she could almost hear them chattering at the end of her consciousness. She'd join the dogwoods, just like her Nana. Later. She smiled as warmth spread through her. They'd embrace her in their creaky limbs and petal-soft blooms.

She'd be ready.

So would the dogwoods.

THE GUARDIAN

Roche Livingston stood on the porch, his stomach tight with the jumble of emotions, bees buzzing in their distress. The old familiar sting of loss welled. Already his hands cramped, a byproduct of how he coped with stress. He forced himself to unclench his fists. He flexed his fingers.

Last week, out of nowhere, Pixie, with her purple hair and magnetic smile, called and coerced him to stop by this, his parents' house. Abandoned house. Left like they would walk back in any second. Pixie had a way of coercing him into unpleasant things to test his bravery, but this was something else.

He turned to the oak front door. The burning fear caused bubbles in his belly. The sight made him suck in his breath to help quell the feeling. When he closed his eyes, he saw the police banging through it to find a murderous and bloody mess. Real panic didn't set in until they'd arrived. He knew then. Something violent happened...

Years ago.

Roche opened his eyes. *Why the hell am I here?*

"You made it!" He jumped, his adrenaline spiking. He turned around to see Pixie pulling into the drive, blowing smoke rings through her open driver's side window.

"Yeah, I did." At the sight of her climbing out of the car, smooth as a black cat slinking along a fence, his stomach did a flip-flop.

She joined him on the stairs. Her purple Bantu knots stood against the chilly breeze. "I wasn't sure you would."

"I really don't want to do this," Roche said. "It's freezing."

Pixie sighed, her friendly smile dissolved, crumbling just like his feelings about being here. He wanted to bring her smile back. Her ray of sunlight warmed him. Even in this dreary place.

"It's been fifteen years, Roche. It's time," Pixie said.

"Time for *what*?"

"To sell it."

"Sell?" Roche's eyebrows rose. *She can't be serious. This place is a murder house!*

"You don't want to spend your life in apartment craptastic, do you?"

"Hey, I like my place." Roche handed her the key and then stepped aside to allow Pixie room to unlock the door. The worn surface bore scratches, gouges, and dings—left-over markings from the police officers' frantic efforts to get inside.

"I couldn't take the chance of you folding like a tent, so I came too." Pixie sighed with the shake of her head. "Come on."

The rush of dust, mildew, and closed-in death rolled out to greet them.

Roche slapped his hand over his mouth and swallowed the awfulness. He cradled his nose in the nook of his elbow with his eyes itching and watering.

"It reeks in here. Damn, I don't wanna chew it." Pixie held her arm up to her face.

"Let's air it out. Leave the door open." Roche pushed ahead. "Remember, you wanted to do this."

They walked into the foyer. Roche stiffened at the place where the area rug used to be. There his dad had lain, a pile of broken bloody pulp. Brutally killed by fists and feet of those who hated and feared what he represented. His mother shot while she slept.

Murder was the ultimate robbery—taking someone's life. Stealing the futures of their loved ones. Forever altering the lives of those who remained.

Furniture still lurked against walls and in corners, covered with sheets, like stationary ghosts anchored to this place. Gloomy reminders of a life cloaked by death and grief.

He was unable to speak, well, not *trusting* himself to say anything more. Roche swallowed the spiky knot of emotion in his throat.

Pixie's sneakers slapped the wood floors as she headed toward the living room. The atmosphere weighed down, thick, heavy, but invisible, like a hand ready to squish them into oblivion.

Roche wiped his damp face. He secured the environment by searching around. His home. Warm and comforted, safe and loved, but now, nothing but a hollow cold that he couldn't blame on the weather.

The methodical practice of getting rid of people came like a scalpel, slicing through lives, leaving scar tissue and anguish behind. Roche continued to be reminded of that vacancy. Mother's Day. Father's Day. Christmas. Each special day would cut open his veins, and he'd bleed out all over again.

He walked to the living room, following the path Pixie had disappeared down seconds before. He found Pixie at the bay window. He stopped.

As teens, Pixie would escape her own home, go to his house, and race through the wide hallways. As she did so, she teased him. Somehow, this helped her ease the horror of living with her uncle, Bobby, and his "hands on" approach to rearing his niece.

But when Pixie tired of all the silliness, she'd stop at this spot, staring out into the distance. Roche often wondered if she peered into the future, to a time when she didn't have to carry such a heavy load of being seen as *fast* as her aunt described her, and *too grown for her own good*, according to her uncle. They sought to stifle the beautiful soul, and they'd almost done it.

Almost.

The dull curtains flickered through her fingers. She puffed out a heavy sigh. Pixie shivered. "Your parents used to hold seances here. That's something we can use to market the house."

Roche snorted. "Not likely. My parents liked the occult. They acknowledged a world beyond what we can see."

Yet something *had* harmed them.

Roche shuddered. A cold sweat came over him. He had to ignore his skin's crawling.

"Well, okay then." Pixie's dark eyes shifted from left to right.

His face felt hot despite the house's chilly temperature. As white, condensed puffs escaped his mouth, he made a right and stopped just outside his bedroom. The walls bore dusty shadows of where posters once hung. Large sheets covered the bulky bedframe and mattress. The bookshelves' corners had collected spider webs and dust bunnies.

"This room looked so much bigger in my mind and memory. Happy hunting, Anazai," Roche said.

Of course, he'd gotten bigger too. Just as he moved to step into the room, he lingered at the threshold, his foot hovering. The room's atmosphere reached outward; its icy and dry fingers flickered through his coat, his sweater, and his undershirt, making him gasp. He fumbled backward, stumbled, and grabbed the wall for stability. Although his body had stopped moving, his heart continued to thunder in terror. Goosebumps broke out over his skin.

"What the heck?" Roche jerked to a fully upright position. He shook himself in a failed attempt to get rid of the chill. Across from him, his bedroom looked the same, a normal room with items left.

He brushed his palms on his jeans. *Could be vertigo.* Every time he traveled, his sinuses and ears had to adjust too, not always in the best way. He released a breath. Yeah, he just had a small moment of vertigo.

Pixie jogged into the hall. "You alright?"

He nodded. "Why?"

"You screamed."

"No, I didn't." Roche looked around. *What had she heard?*

"Dude, you totally did. What, you run into a spider or cockroach?"

"Don't even joke about roaches." His voice held an edge of warning. The sharp memory of him eating a bowl of raisin cereal and some of the dark pieces moving against the brown flakes made his skin crawl.

Pixie shrugged. "Okay. But don't be embarrassed. I *know* I heard something."

"Nah. I'm not, but I didn't."

Pixie smirked, as if she knew better.

"This your old room, huh?" She turned into the bedroom, passing through the doorway without incident.

Maybe he'd imagined it.

Shaking off the memory, Roche followed Pixie into his former living space. Those ghosts of his childhood remained, floating through the confined space, but he bit the inside of his cheek. Nothing came whirling out at him, so maybe earlier *had been* vertigo.

"Wow. You had your own room. I forgot that. Tina and I had to share." Shadows clung to her face. Watery light streamed in through the sole window's blinds. They hadn't been completely closed.

Pixie roamed the room, peering at each of the dust-covered whatnots, old handheld games, and former book favorites. Unlike the living room, this space had remained untouched

"What's this?" Pixie squatted down in front of his three-tier shelves. She dug deep into the middle shelf and retrieved something from its bowels. She opened her palm and revealed a black glass sea turtle. She blew the dust off. "Cute little thing."

"That's a guardian." Roche broke out in a sweat. He swallowed to ease his dry throat. He pointed and noticed his index finger trembling. His momma had warned him not to move it from his room. She believed it would keep his nightmares, both real and imagined, away. "Put it back."

He didn't know why he knew that, but parts of his childhood remained covered and cloaked like the pieces of furniture in the living room. Not that the thing had protected his parents from a violent and bloody death, but still. His mother had warned him to leave the guardians alone. They'd been placed all over the house. The one assigned to him had been this turtle.

"Why? It's cute." Pixie straightened and dropped it in her coat's pocket. "I'll clean it up, and it can guard my apartment."

"No. No. Put it back. I'm serious." Roche tried to retrieve the totem from her pocket without success. For a few minutes, they wrestled, Pixie twisting this way and that to keep Roche from reclaiming what she valued now as hers. Roche's frustration fed grunts and hard snatches against Pixie's coat, arms, and hands as she tried to get away.

"Ow! You're hurting me!" Pixie pushed him. "Get. Off!"

A few tense moments stretched out between them. After a forced parting, they glared at each other. This strange game of chicken ended when Pixie broke eye contact.

"Just put it back," Roche grunted before turning away.

His stomach rumbled, and his knees buckled. He caught himself before hitting the ground, but the pain ricocheted up to his thighs. A crippling agony kept him down, cheek pressed against the cool, wooden floor. Tears pooled in the corners of his eyes. His nose burned. His skin sizzled.

What the hell is happening?

Pixie leaned over him. Concern crinkled her delicate features. It shone bright in her face, illuminating the fear.

"Ro? You okay?"

"No," seethed out through his clenched teeth.

"What's wrong?" She squatted down beside him, her sneakers squeaking against the flooring.

"Don't touch me!" He waved his hands to ward her off.

Pixie scrambled backward.

"Put... It... Back!" Roche spat, tongue swollen. Maybe if she put the guardian back in its place, he could get off the floor.

With eyes wide with fear, Pixie fished around in her coat pocket. She took the turtle and placed it on the bookshelf. "Are you serious?"

The wave of agony receded. The hot flames cooled. The cramping eased. Roche pushed up on his palms and let out a sense of relief.

"You're so dramatic," Pixie said with another side-eyed glare. "You really are something." She shook her head and crossed her arms. "For real, tho?"

Roche got slowly to his knees and then his feet. The remnants of pain lingered like little numbing shots of ice-cold and aches in the back of his head. "You think I faked that?"

"Hell yeah, you faked it! Throwing a tantrum to get your way." Pixie cocked her head.

"I didn't fake it. Something hit me like a fist, just now, and now it's gone." Roche shuffled away from the room. "I dunno."

"You don't know?" Pixie followed behind him, her words thrown against his back.

Had it been a coincidence? The pain hurt, and it started the moment Pixie picked up the turtle. He pushed the feeling aside. He couldn't fully engage those superstitions. Once he got time, he could get online and spend the night and early morning slaying demons, wraiths, and other-worldly monsters.

"Leave it!" Roche said. It came out more harshly than necessary. Pixie flinched, but didn't come at him again.

He had to get out of here. Returning had been a mistake. "I don't care what happens to this hellish place."

Pixie stopped short. "I guess we can always come back tomorrow. This house would net a good price. Four bedrooms, the acreage…"

"…and the triple homicides," Roche finished. He paused, his hand on the front doorknob. "Robby didn't even get to turn thirteen, Pix."

"I know." A sadness fluttered across her face. "This house is your birthright."

"Birthright? They're *all* dead!" Roche whirled around, hands clenched in fists.

"Yes, but you aren't." Pixie stood, arms akimbo.

"Yeah." Roche zipped his coat. He'd been at school, blissfully unaware and bored out of his mind. This wasn't the Pixie he remembered. She'd changed somehow. Sure, her life had been hard, but whose hadn't? He'd changed too.

Without another word, he left. The moment he reached the porch, an immediate weight fell from his shoulders. Now that he discovered the house hadn't changed, bile pressed—hot and bitter—against the back of his throat. He punched his thigh with his fist. Why had he let Pixie drag him out here? All they managed to do was dredge up the vile past. His therapist said the past remained unchanged, so he might as well focus on the present.

For half a beat, he thought about waiting for Pixie before marching down the stairs and out into the chilly late day.

PIXIE WATCHED ROCHE LEAVE WITH HER HOPE, sinking with each loud *thunk* of his boots. She sighed. *That didn't go according to plan.*

Roche's living conditions appalled her. His apartment couldn't be a long-term residence. She retreated into the foyer, shutting the door behind her. Roche would be back. That filthy box he lived in didn't constitute a house or residence, only a mere dwelling. He deserved more, because, well, he made sure *she* had more.

He was a fire hydrant of fury. Sure, the murders were terrible, but ancient knowledge. She made her way back to the warmer sections of the house—the parts the weak sun had showered with sunlight earlier today. She found herself drawn again to Roche's bedroom. The room pulsated, like a bloody heart. When she raised her hand, palm out, a rush of warm air rushed out to greet it. A chill skated up her arm.

Maybe Roche didn't fake it. He did used to prank her a lot when they were younger, but now that she thought about it, he had looked pained.

The electric hadn't been turned on in the house. The rest of the residence remained ice cold. Frowning, Pixie stepped into the room, the atmosphere wrapped around her. It brought up gooseflesh. A fluttering started in her belly. At that moment, she felt like she'd stepped outside her body, and watched as the other Pixie squatted down in front of the bookshelf, her hand outstretched toward the black, glass turtle.

Roche's words wiggled back to her. *"It's a guardian."*

A guardian? It hadn't guarded the Livingstons' home from a triple murder. So, maybe it wasn't that kind of guardian, but it meant a lot to Roche. It had to for him to act a plum fool.

A faint tinning interrupted the quiet. Before she could even determine the source, the room started to close in. The walls shrank in increments, like the room breathed. With each breath, the walls constricted, coming closer.

Pixie yelped and raced out of the room, down the hall-way, through the living room, and out the front door. When she got to her car, she stopped, bent over, snatching as much oxygen as she could for her starved lungs, heart thundering as if it had decided *not* to stop.

"What the entire fuck?" She looked as the front door, which she had wrenched wide, swung shut with a loud *thwack*. She jumped again. "Fuck!"

"It must've been the wind," she whispered.

Her angst at the day's ruin, Roche's leaving, and her own temporary terror made her shiver. She closed her eyes and breathed deep. When she exhaled, she slowly opened her eyes. The front door remained unlocked.

She sat in the cold front seat. If she left it unlocked, vagrants could squat inside the house, and if she wanted to help Roche get it on the market, she couldn't leave it open. Her fingers ached from gripping the steering wheel. One last thing and then she could go home.

"The wind. That's all, just the damn wind," she muttered as she stalked back up the stairs to lock the door.

She couldn't stop her hands from shaking. "Just cold. They're just cold."

No sounds. No birds. No cicada. Total silence. Nothing. No signs of life. It left her shaken, so she hurried back down the stairs.

Pixie rushed to her car. Once inside, she pulled a cigarette from her pack and stuck it in her mouth. She'd never needed one more than she did right now. Tomorrow, she'd start trying to quit again. Once she started the car, she fumbled around in her pocket for her lighter, and her fingertips brushed something smooth and cold. She froze. Slowly, she removed her hand and looked in her other pocket for her lighter. The chill skating up her back had nothing to do with the cold. After all, she'd turned on the car's heater and locked the doors.

"There!" she shouted as she pulled out her slick metal lighter. She hastily lit her cigarette and tried to focus on the task of leaving. Now. She buckled her seatbelt and put the car in reverse.

Once she reached the highway, she relaxed, but only a little bit. She took a drag, long and deep, before expelling the smoke. She switched on her music, and the soulfulness slid from the speakers. Pixie let out a breath.

Her cellphone buzzed. Roche's name flickered across the car's Bluetooth display.

She answered. "What?"

"Pix? Look, about today..."

Pixie cut through his whining apology before he dispersed it. "Why am I here? What's the point? Nothing I do really matters."

"I know, and I'm grateful. I swear I am," Roche said, his voice small.

Pixie sighed. She reached a stoplight. He didn't really know. Did he understand that she felt like a ghost? Empty. Vacant of any real substance. He didn't know how she stood in front of her bedroom mirror and dragged the razorblade across her forearm, watched the crimson liquid well up and then race down to her hands. Proof that she was alive, that she existed, and that she had *life*.

No, Roche didn't know shit.

"What do you want?" Even to her ears, she sounded exhausted and mean. She took another cigarette out of the packet and waited for the light to change. Was he on the way back to Chicago?

"Look, I'm sorry. I'm just not in a good place."

"I'm sorry, too. I freaked out earlier. Being back here called up all my anxieties."

The traffic light turned green, and Pixie continued through the intersection. She fished around her coat pocket for her lighter when her fingers brushed that cold, smooth surface again.

"What is this?" she mumbled around the cigarette dangling from her lips. She snatched it out, her curiosity exasperating her patience.

"Pix? Did you hear me?"

Roche sounded a million miles away, down a long tunnel. Pixie opened her hand, and to her absolute horror, the black glass turtle moved across her palm.

"How the hell?" Pixie asked, a few moments before the blaring of car horns snatched her attention to back to the road.

Ahead, a stopped pickup truck, trapped in her headlights like a frightened deer, its scarlet brake lights illuminated against the dark ground, didn't move. Pixie slammed on her own brakes, praying no one rear-ended her, and in turn, that she didn't ram into the back of the truck.

She shut her eyes and shrieked.

"Pix! Pix!" Roche shouted into the cellphone. Her screaming ripped across his belly, and all his butterflies escaped in a flutter. Adrenaline exploded inside him. "Shit! Pix!"

He disconnected the call, grabbed his coat, snatching it on as he collected his car keys and hotel room key. Already shaking from the sudden shot of adrenaline and terror, Roche spat out the nasty taste in his mouth. "Please be okay."

The echo of Pixie's cries, set on repeat, continued playing in his mind. He left the room, almost running down the hallway and out to the hotel parking lot. The roar of an ambulance, and later the sirens of the police car seemingly chasing it, ratcheted up his fear. He started his rental car, a huge boxy thing with boring gray tires.

He had no idea where Pixie was heading. He scanned the streets for the ambulance and police cars that had raced by him. The pit in his stomach rolled into a knot, tightening with each mile he drove.

He took out his phone. "Call Pixie."

His Bluetooth connected the call. Ringing.

Hope ignited in him when her voice greeted him in an amazing professional and crisp. "Hello—"

"Pix! Where are you?"

"I'm currently unable to take your call. Please leave me a message or text me and I will get back to you as soon as I can. Bye."

The voicemail's beep slapped him in the face. "Damn it, Pix, call me back."

At once, forces that seemed to pull from the center of the earth beneath his vehicle shook him, shoving him off into a ditch. Roche couldn't say it was the wind, because nothing moved except his car. As if a giant hand pushed his toy truck into the trench.

"Hey buddy! You need some help?" called a white man. He'd already pulled off the road behind Roche and was getting out of his car.

"No. I'm fine!" Fear crawled over Roche, a thousand needles of worry. He didn't want a white man on the side of the road with him this late at night. It wasn't safe. He didn't want his dead body lying alongside his sedan.

The man hesitated. "You sure? I can call 911."

"No, I'm fine. I—I've already called a tow truck!" He waited until the man pulled back onto the road before turning his attention to the field attached to the ditch. The police didn't see life and death, only offenses and dark brown skin. Nope, he didn't need that drama tonight.

Blackness reached out across the land, but overhead, stars shone, free from the clouds that had cloaked their presence earlier in the day. He reached into his backpack and took out his flashlight. Dread piled into his stomach, but

Roche started walking toward the field's center. A numb feeling draped him. His feet moved of their own accord, possessed by something unfamiliar to him, and yet strangely calming. A warmth pooled at his feet and spiraled up his legs, like one of those pedicure water massages. He kept walking, pulled by some invisible force, which guided each step.

As he kept walking, the grass, parched by winter, crunched under his boots. He spied the hood of the car, a bright yellow like Pixie's little Mazda hatchback. He tried to hurry, but his body didn't go any faster. His heart raced. He couldn't control his body, just like earlier at the house. Sweat broke out across his forehead. With as much strength as he could muster, he tried to stop. His muscles burned as he pressed forward, the muscles disobeying. The furious feeling of urgency to reach Pixie.

Roche's eyes watered from the effort of trying to stop. When at last he crested the small incline, Pixie's car came into view again. Once he crossed the field's center, he stumbled as something pushed him.

"Oh!" His arms windmilled as he regained command over his body. He exhaled and wiped his brow. A strong shiver raced across him. He checked out the vehicle, walking around it, peeking in windows, and trying the doors—which he found locked.

But where was she?

No structures. No other vehicles. It was like something scooped up Pixie's car and set it down here, in this spot. His flashlight, turned searchlight, didn't reveal any signs of tire tracks or flattened winter grass.

"Pixie!" he shouted, using his flashlight to cut through the thick darkness. "Pixie, you here?"

Nothing.

Something bumped into his boot. Roche shouted and pointed light in that direction. At his feet was a turtle, as black as the night, blending into the darkness. The hairs on the back of his neck rose in silent alarm.

"What the hell?" He slowly inched his flashlight across the ground.

Another equally inky dark turtle. Then another. And another. Roche realized he had been surrounded by scores of black, glossy turtles as his flashlight revealed more of them. It reminded him of those nature hiccups where a beach is covered with dead whales or a swarm of butterflies blots out the sky or a sidewalk is filled with frogs. Abnormal incidents of nature, some with causes, some without.

This *definitely* didn't have a cause.

Not a natural one.

He took a steadying breath and squatted down for a better look. The closest turtle's shell glistened like rain against asphalt. Black. Not green. Not dirty. No, a solid black creature—eyes, feet, shell, everything. It didn't seem dead, but it didn't seem to be alive either. It just sat there. Asleep? Were they all asleep?

The others appeared to be in similar stasis.

Roche shuddered. The view freaked him out and reminded him of a thousand black beetles scattered across a desk. Surreal and sinister, the silence made him uncomfortable.

A putrid odor flooded the area. Roche coughed. He'd smelled that awfulness before—his house. Death. A rush of bile and early supper spewed from his lips so fast it shot through his nose, too. Although he tried to avoid the turtles, he couldn't, and the *splat* against their shells made him sick all over again. He stepped back and wiped his mouth with the back of his hand.

As he did so, a scuttling sound rose up fast against the thick quiet. With a quick flick of his wrist, the light landed on a figure not more than ten feet away. The motionless turtles had awakened. They moved, surprisingly fast, toward the figure. To Roche's horror, they didn't stop at the shadow figure's feet, but crawled onto it. They kept coming, blackened shimmering shells piling on like roaches scurrying over rotting meat.

Repulsed, Roche turned away. He'd call the police and pray that if they found Pixie, they wouldn't shoot her on sight. The slithering noise of the turtles moving against each other made his skin crawl. The cool night air remained still, as if awaiting the next horrible action. God forgive him. Every inch of him stood taut with fear and trembling with terror. He took one step and realized he couldn't take another. His hands shook and his legs had gone numb, weakened by uncertainty.

He'd lost control of his muscles and limbs again. Unable to stop himself, he turned back to the now enormous...being in front of him. He moved the flashlight toward the sky. Roche couldn't believe his eyes. Thousands of turtles' flippers moved in sync. A wet noise squished continuously, and the swell of sour ocean water hung thick in the air.

The odor made Roche want to vomit again. His empty stomach lurched.

"What are you?" he shouted. Surprised he could talk, he added, "Where's Pixie?"

"I am a Guardian." The voice sounded like a chorus of screeching whales.

Somehow, Roche understood it. The unsettled feeling he felt earlier in the house came roaring back, and he fell to his knees. Like an ice pick through his skull, a sharp pain pierced his head. He shrieked and his ears ached from the thunderous sound.

"Guardian," Roche said, peering through slits, his eyes watering at the pungent odor and the indignity. Roche laughed. The guffaw exploded from his mouth at the ridiculousness. This giant turtle comprised of thousands of other turtles speaking without lips, considered itself a guardian. Like the cheap glass one from his bedroom? It didn't protect anything.

The turtle's rigid mouth opened again.

"You left them unprotected. You carried me in your pocket to school," the Guardian explained.

A flash of crippling electricity shot through Roche. He winced in agony. Images pierced his mind, his memory restored in icepick stabs.

His momma warning him to leave the turtle alone.

Him slipping the turtle into his pocket and fleeing the room.

Him showing it to Pixie at school during lunch.

Him coming home to the rotating lights of blue and scarlet.

Scarlet.

Everywhere.

"Stop!" Roche roared. His throat burned. He wiped his face and realized he'd been crying this entire time. Snot ran down his lips and mixed with tears.

The guardian's silence offered some relief from the pain.

"Where's Pixie?" Roche asked, his heart hurting.

The mountain of turtles shifted, and the ground shook. The turtles that formed the beak opened, but they grew longer and wider, forming stairs. The endless squirming turtles awaited.

Roche frowned. He tried to sit up and realized he could move his body. He let out a big breath, breathed in, and gagged on the odor. When he looked up, he couldn't quite wrap his mind around the situation.

"Come."

Roche shuddered.

Here, the putrid odor intensified, but Roche held it together, his stomach doing somersaults.

Somewhere inside the mass of writhing turtles, Pixie remained. She might be trapped. She might be hurt. He couldn't let her down again, not like the time when they were kids, and he left her to be bullied by his friends. He focused on the pain. The mass looked exactly like the miniature turtle from his bedroom, albeit distorted. The Guardian looked ready to burst., swollen with hundreds of wiggling turtles. This opportunity could help him fill the hole grief had torn inside him.

He stepped onto the first turtle while reaching overhead to grab the next hardened shell to hoist himself up. Roche began climbing, not looking down, and not breathing through his nose. His arms ached, his lower back burned, but he kept going. *Pixie needs me.*

Once he reached the Guardian's chin, Roche paused. His breathing labored, and his blood pounding in his ears, he held his position. He needed to get into the Guardian's mouth to gain access to the body, because somewhere in there Pixie remained, but then what? Would it consume him? Render him tonight's bloody snack?

Beneath the stains of time, the truth had always lingered like a lump deep in his gut.

The Guardian required sacrifice for his lack of faith. His parents and brother had been payment before, and now, it required his own to save Pixie.

Warm air wrapped around him, binding him as the turtles' flippers pushed him toward the closing mouth. He held himself still as the wave of turtles pushed him higher. He didn't dare look for fear he'd be seduced into flinging himself over the edge to kill the horror haunting him.

As he ascended, he started to wheeze. Vertigo threatened to overwhelm him. The nausea rushed through him. The acidic taste coated his tongue. He wouldn't let Pixie down.

Not again.

Not ever.

The warm, rancid odor intensified, and his throat closed. He squeezed his eyes shut, but the Guardian's image fixed in his mind, infiltrating his eyelids and standing impossibly tall.

Before his courage leaked out, Roche hoisted himself further into the Guardian's mouth.

Soon the warmth melted into sizzling heat, burning his skin, as if his entire body had been set on fire.

Roche lost consciousness.

RELIVED THAT HE WAS ALIVE, ROCHE OPENED HIS eyes. He spied the oversized leg of what appeared to be a nightstand. He glanced around, but realized his stiff neck didn't allow free range of motion. When he lifted his hand, he found it to be a flipper. Roche opened his mouth to scream, but nothing came out. Panic flooded his heart. He tried to move his legs, his feet, anything. Nothing worked.

Am I paralyzed?

"There you are!" Pixie exclaimed. "I don't know how you got in my pocket yesterday, but here you are."

She was giant, almost as large as the Guardian, as she scooped him up into her palm. He wanted to smile, but again, his facial muscles couldn't move. A small head wound spoke of what was probably her car accident. As she moved around what must be her room, the realization dawned on him. He had shrunk.

"Roche went back to his craptastic apartment, I guess. He won't return my calls, but you're my keepsake from him."

I haven't gone anywhere. I'm right here! Roche thought.

Pixie walked over to her mirror and she placed him down. As she fixed her hair, Roche spied himself in the mirror. Glistening outer shell, snapping mouth, and dark beady eyes all appeared both foreign and familiar. Where once he had arms and legs, there had been rendered flippers and a tiny tail.

"I feel so safe with you here," Pixie said. "I like that you're guarding me."

As the stinging horror faded, Roche realized he'd never let Pixie down again.

He'd guard her for life.

TURN OF THE LEAF

Sunlight heated the concrete and surrounding brick buildings in Beacon Homes, turning it into one hell of a neighborhood pressure cooker. Folks' tempers had been burnt to short, frayed ends. People could fry eggs and meth on the sidewalks. Oscar Banks rounded the curve, nostrils flared, running full out with legs pumping and heart heaving down Magnolia Avenue, through the Beacon's belly. The rec center sat in the community's guts. It fed the youth's interest in sports, cards, and music.

"Ay, O! Slow down!" someone shouted as he streaked past.

The pounding rhythm filled Oscar's ears. He glanced in the caller's direction for a second before pushing on up the small hill to Badgett Avenue. There, he'd be able to escape.

Freedom awaited—a glistening light slicing through the darkness.

Badgett Avenue snaked around Beacon Homes like an invisible wall. Funny thing about Beacon, it didn't have houses, only apartments. Probably why they called it *Homes* and not Beacon *Houses*. The actual buildings shared concrete porches with those next door. Across from Beacon Homes, a row of real houses alternated between shotgun and single-story. They glared in full superiority to the zero rent *apartments*.

Something glinted, catching the sun's beam. It winked at Oscar and forced him to raise his hand to shield his eyes.

"Time to get up." Aunt Shirley flicked the light switch two more times, creating a brief disco effect in the gloomy bedroom. "You got work."

Oscar's heart raced, thudding against his fingertips. His sweatpants plastered to his legs from sweat. He wiped the perspiration from his forehead but wiped his chest with the thin and damp sheet.

He closed his eyes, opened them, and gathered his bearings.

Window. Shade. Side table. Mat. Home.

He untied his durag and scratched his head.

"Aight." He threw back the faded green sheet.

"Put a shirt on." Aunt Shirley left.

The cold linoleum floor made his bare feet ache, so he hurried to pull on socks. The walls failed to keep winter at bay. He could see his breath. When he padded out to the hallway, he found his aunt standing in front of the linen closet.

"The heat off?" Oscar asked.

"It's broken. Called them people to come fix it." Aunt Shirley tugged her scarf down over the tips of her ears. Gray bangs hung over her forehead, brushing her square glasses. She wore a faded purple bathrobe, gray sweatpants, and wool socks. "They said they workin' on it."

Oscar nodded, indicating he heard her.

He shuffled to the bathroom. Once inside, he locked the door and set about brushing his teeth. He picked the blue toothbrush, rinsed it with hot water, and then added a smear of toothpaste. Aunt Shirley didn't like waste.

As soon as Oscar turned on the tap, a death-like gurgle sounded from deep in the pipes. A mournful melody rose to the ceiling, prickling his skin and warming it against the chilly interior. It tugged on his memory.

"Shit!"

He hurried to shut off the tap but dropped his tooth-brush. It clattered and splattered toothpaste against the linoleum.

The music stopped.

A tense quiet followed.

Oscar cracked open the bathroom door and looked down the hall.

Did Aunt Shirley hear that?

No one came running to admonish him or fuss about the loud music first thing in the morning. He closed the door and picked up his toothbrush. Hair and dust bunnies clung to it. Oscar looked at the faucet and then back to his toothbrush.

He reached out to turn on the hot water again. His hand hovered over the dial.

"Nah, it's all up here. Get it together, O."

He released a deep breath and turned on the tap.

As the water spurted out, the dense strings of violins vibrated in concert. The song blared, shaking the window. Oscar shoved his toothbrush beneath the water trickling from the faucet. With his ear full of melody, he thumbed off the dirt and then brushed his teeth as fast as he could.

Several hard knocks broke the swirling tune in time to Oscar turning off the water. The doorknob rattled.

"Yeah?"

"Hurry up!" Aunt Shirley said.

"Yes, ma'am." Oscar slipped the toothbrush into its holder, wiped his hands on his sweats, and unlocked the door.

"You still have white stuff all over your mouth." Aunt Shirley pointed at his lips and made an imaginary circle. "I told you to put a shirt on."

"Yeah, I know. It sounds like you have to go right now. If you don't, though, I can go back in..." Oscar stepped backward.

"Stop playing, boy!" Aunt Shirley swatted him and lumbered inside, slamming the door behind her.

He waited until he heard the toilet flushing. The splashing of water and the soft rumble of the pipes spoke to Aunt Shirley washing her hands.

No music.

He frowned. Ever since his mom died, he'd been prone to random bouts of music. The genres came from all over, like when he and his mom used to listen to the radio, turning the dial to muffle the violent poverty of loud, angry arguments, growling bellies, and wailing children.

They'd lie on the threadbare carpet in the small living room, on their backs, letting the music pour over them. After she died, his Aunt Shirley took him in. She didn't like the radio and the devil's music. She called it sinful.

"Why you standing there? You ain't got work?" Aunt Shirley shooed him away from the door and stood at the threshold with her hands on her hips and her eyebrows in her gray hair.

"Yes, ma'am. Slow moving," Oscar muttered.

He went into his bedroom and raised the window's shade. Weak light filtered in. Its watery beam rippled across his pile of clothes. They hugged each other, clasping each article to form a makeshift support for him to sleep on.

Oscar thought back to the faucet. The melody tasted familiar, but it faded as soon as he thought of it, evaporating out of his reach. He pulled on his work pants, a long-sleeved shirt, and his gray hoodie. The work boots bore rips and tears along the sides. He tied the laces in double knots to keep them from flopping when he walked.

His mother had drowned in the local community pool. The lifeguards—two—were too busy at first. One argued with a teenager about his tomfoolery in the deep end. The second one had to assist a toddler left unattended who'd wandered into the big people's pool, in search of his daddy.

Not now. Work. Gotta work.

He ran a pick through his hair, careful not to untangle his tight curls. When he emerged from his bedroom, he found Aunt Shirley hovering near the front door.

"Aren't you a little old to be working there? I thought only the little ones did sneaker work." Aunt Shirley brushed debris off one of his hoodie's arms.

Oscar shook his head. "It pays. Big. Little. They want product out fast. Job security."

"They payin' both of y'all the same?" She frowned.

"They payin'." Oscar fished out a crinkled envelope with scarlet smears along the edge. "Here."

"What's this?" Aunt Shirley took it.

"Bills."

"This it?" Aunt Shirley's eyebrows rose into her bangs. She thumbed through the crumpled bills.

"Mores comin'." Oscar jerked his hoodie down over his skinny waist.

Aunt Shirley pressed her lips. "They keep raisin' the price on what we need to live and lowerin' it on our lives. I heard on the news we expected to live to 63. Used to be 70. It's a shame. Folks' lives be cheap as toilet paper at the bus station."

"I gotta go."

"It's freezing out. I got an extra sweater..."

"No problem."

OSCAR CROSSED MAGNOLIA AVENUE ON THE WAY to the bus stop. Public transportation didn't come to Beacon Homes. Neither did pizza delivery, but folks didn't have extra money for it, anyway. Not many had cars. If Beacon Homes residents wanted to escape, they had to work at it.

Claw.

Crawl.

Creep.

A loose huddle of men hugged a metal trashcan fire. The fire pit smoldered just like them, burning in their rage, faces glowering at all the injustice and indifference, reflecting the flames flickering for answers, salvation.

"Ain't you cold?" one of them called out to Oscar.

"We freezin'. You ain't freezin', bruh?"

Truth was Oscar's nose, hands, and feet were numb from cold. His needed to work to keep him moving. Positions at the sneaker factory didn't come often. He'd been lucky enough to get on.

Oscar crossed the street, pushing past *BHomes* emblazed on brick walls in bright red. Residents tagged the structures to claim ownership with paint but never with ink. The graffiti followed Oscar right up to Hampton Avenue where it stopped, unable to cross the street outside the neighborhood.

The throng gathered around the bus stop, grunted at each other in greeting.

"Cold this morning," one of them said.

Murmured feedback replied like the rolling static from an amp. Oscar hunched back into his hoodie and stood outside the loose circle of pedestrians. His hand brushed something warm.

"Oh! Hi!" A woman with large, owl-like eyes the color of syrup waved a hand. "Sorry about that. I was searching for meaning."

Oscar inched back. "No problem."

The rail-thin woman stepped forward, blinking behind big, round glasses. Her green peacoat had the collar turned up with a crimson scarf. Her dark skin shined against her gold-toned hoop earrings. "You come here every morning."

"Yeah. Work." Oscar shoved his hands into his pockets.

"I see." She flapped her arms, creating a space around her. Others shifted to avoid being struck. A green shoulder strap slid down her arm. She slipped it back into place. "I'm Birdie."

"Oscar."

"Nice to meet you, Oscar."

The conversation died beneath the arriving bus's wheels.

A red-faced bus driver slammed the door open and beckoned them to board. They climbed in, single file, each depositing dollars into the container. Oscar fished out three. They bore scarlet smears along the edge. He dropped them in with the others, and took his seat, a few rows behind the driver.

Once all had boarded, the red-faced driver closed the door. Birdie took the seat across the aisle from Oscar. Other passengers disappeared into their devices.

"Next stop, Montgomery!"

The bus lunged forward, pulling out into the dark morning street.

"You like where you work?" Birdie reached across and touched Oscar's knee.

"It's just work." Oscar shrunk back, fleeing contact, connection.

"Does it bring you pleasure?" Birdie tilted her head and peered at him. She folded her hands over her purse nestled in her lap.

"It pays the bills."

Birdie faced the front. "Bills. Humph. Animals live for free. They eat what they want, find their shelter for free..."

"Shit wherever..." someone added from the rear.

"We ain't animals!" shouted another.

Birdie twisted in her seat to face the hecklers. "Certain things should be *free*. Food, shelter, healthcare should be provided for all people."

"Sex! That should be free, too," the heckler cackled.

"That is free, though."

"Not if you're single."

"You ain't doin' right if it ain't free..."

Oscar gazed out the window. Their words buzzed like bothersome flies.

"Montgomery! All you in the back, pipe down!" The driver pulled over to the curb. He glared through the over-sized rearview mirror. "Or you get off here."

Several people exited.

Once the bus resumed its path down Hampton Avenue, Birdie turned to Oscar.

"I'm sorry. The conversation wasn't ladylike," she said.

"No problem." Oscar spied the sneaker factory looming in the distance.

The early morning dark hid most of the building's girth, but not its billowing white smoke. It belched into the air from four brick stacks. Though it evaporated fast, the thick smoke appeared solid. These puffs were the first thing Oscar saw as the bus approached each morning as if messaging him to come hither.

The factory sign was the other.

Glowing in bright, white Times New Roman font, the sign served as a beacon in a sea of blackness above the factory's entrance.

Here was salvation.

"Chicago Avenue!"

"It was nice meeting you." Birdie pulled her purse strap over her shoulder and left via the rear exit.

It wasn't until the bus had gone another block down the road that Oscar realized he was cold.

"Scarlet Drive!"

Oscar disembarked and headed to the sneaker factory's front entrance. His stomach rumbled in reminder.

"Need to eat."

The factory horn blared. Workers' silhouettes shuffled through the gate, like dead men walking, talking among themselves with hushed tones. An acid taste coated Oscar's tongue. The taste of the factory.

All the walking caused sweat to pool around Oscar's collar. A thin layer of perspiration slid down his neck, dripped onto his chest. He made a beeline for the breakroom. He picked up a cup to get water from the sink. With his jaw tense and tightened, Oscar approached the faucet. Dried saliva irritated his throat. He looked over his shoulder and searched around behind him.

No one entered.

Oscar gripped the metal sink with damp hands. His veins bulged and throbbed. His fingernails dug into the steel, the cold and damp seeped up his fingers, into his palms. A handle on the faucet was missing. Two spots above it, from where the handle should have been, was a pair of pliers. The mirror was cracked.

An eerie hush hung in the breakroom's dry heat.

Oscar squeezed his eyes shut, clenched his teeth, and smelled the dust of the factory floor, the machinery oil. His nostrils flared. Breath quivered between his lips. He stood on his toes, his body caught between thirst and flight.

Drawing his lip back, he found it dry and cracked, not a single hint of saliva to fill its cracks.

The paper cup's lip widened. As it grew, so did Oscar's ache. Before his courage failed him, he twisted the nozzle with the pliers.

Water flowed, smacking the cup's bottom, and sloshed onto his hands. The cold shocked him and he lost his grip. He recovered and managed to get a few swallows of water.

Not that he noticed due to the blaring, fast-paced techno music whirling around him. Oscar winced at the volume and scrambled to turn the tap off.

Panting, Oscar searched the breakroom. The hairs on the back of his neck stood in protest. His heart pounded, and droplets of cold sweat raced down his face. He wiped them with the back of his hand.

The door to the breakroom burst open and in rushed the roar of machinery.

"Ay, you coming to work or what?" The line supervisor stuck his head into the room.

Oscar jumped.

"Get your ass in gear!"

When the warning horn blared, it shook the factory floor and caused dust to rain down from the ceiling. The factory was a hive of activity, each level a different task and vibe. Oscar opened his mouth, and his breath filled his ears. The swishing of his hand through his pocket to retrieve his candy bar, the thumping of his heart, and his shallow breath sucking through his nostrils set him askew. The ringing of metal and the creaking of a factory floor filled his head where rapid music had been seconds before.

Oscar unwrapped the candy bar and crammed it into his mouth. He washed it down with the rest of the water in the cup.

The workday waited for no one.

A SIREN RANG THROUGH THE CITY, A REMINDER OF what happened to those who tried to escape.

"Move it!" the bus driver shouted into her radio.

Her horn blared as the car in front of her inched ahead. The cars behind her leaned on their horns in protest. The static from the radio garbled, barely audible through the racket. Her braids flapped as she turned to see if everyone was present.

Oscar sat still, waiting for the next stoplight. He stared out the window, letting his mind wander. The neon signs of bars and fast-food joints blurred into distractions. The only thing of note was the brick walls lining the street. Shadows cast along them once the sun was gone, but they shouted messages like physical SOS signals.

He stuffed his hands into his hoodie's pockets.

The watery sun hugged the horizon on its way down for the night.

"Chicago Avenue!"

The front door slapped open. Birdie climbed the three flat stairs and deposited her crisp three bills into the container. She sat across the aisle from him. As the bus resumed, she turned to him.

"Hi." She pushed her glasses up the bridge of her nose. "Good day?"

"Hi." Oscar turned away from the window to face her.

"I'm guessing you aren't having a good day." She tilted her head sideways.

Oscar fidgeted in the chair, trying to get more comfortable. "I can't complain about my job. It's work."

"Sure, but are you saying you don't know?"

He shrugged.

She leaned forward, her purse tucked in her lap. "You flinched when I spoke to you."

His cheeks burned; he could feel heat, so he yanked the hoodie's collar forward.

Birdie opened her mouth, but before she could speak, he sucked in a breath, and said, "I thought you had somethin' to tell me..."

His voice trailed off as he drowned in his own words, rubbing his face with his hands as he tried to gather the detached thoughts that had been coursing through the day.

At the sound of her laughter, he looked up. Her eyes were bright; they danced over his face and lips, stopping at his eyes and sweeping down again. Her laugh was warm and melodic, and she reached out and touched his knee as she continued laughing.

He stiffened.

She pulled her hand back. "I didn't mean to scare you."

He could feel himself blush all over again—whether from embarrassment or excitement, he couldn't tell.

Birdie sat up straight. "Can I invite you out for a drink? There's a place near the Montgomery stop that closes at nine."

Oscar looked into Birdie's soft brown eyes. Fires ignited in his soul. A warmth melted through his spine and into his chest. It spread up his neck, over his cheeks, and lifted his mouth in a smile.

His voice sounded far away when he said, "Sure."

THE CAFE'S SOFT LIGHTING PRODUCED SHADOWS. They lingered in corners and under tables. Birdie approached the counter, ordered a black coffee, and then turned to Oscar with her eyebrows raised in question.

"What do you want?"

Oscar had no idea. No one had asked him that before.

"Whatever you get."

Birdie turned to the server. "He'll have hot chocolate." With a glance over her shoulder, she said to Oscar, "You look like you need something sweet."

Oscar glided over to two chairs and a table near the window. He eased down into the seat facing the door, with the wall to his back, and the window on his left.

The afternoon sun sank, and with it any residual warmth. Pedestrians outside puffed out breaths and clutched coats close to their bodies as if they could hold on to heat.

"Here you go." Birdie put the mug down in front of him and sat across.

He wrapped both his hands around its base.

"Careful, it's hot." Birdie nodded at the steam. "You don't wanna scald yourself like that woman at the fast-food place. Third-degree burns all over her thighs and stomach."

Oscar turned to look out the window. He spied Birdie peering at him in the reflection. She took tiny quick sips of her coffee. The *zzrup* reminded him of flies buzzing in the kitchen during the summer. The project's bricks burned so hot, folks fried eggs on the sidewalk, and dared each other to eat them. Flies weren't so picky.

"It's Oscar. Right?" Birdie chirped.

"Yeah."

"I'm Birdie. I'm not sure you remembered from earlier."

"Yeah, I remember."

"Really? I was hoping you would've forgotten."

Oscar frowned, his palms sweating.

"So, um, you like your job?" Birdie asked.

He forced a smile, squinting. "I guess."

"You guess?"

Oscar turned away from the window, his face hot. He scooted his hot chocolate away.

"How long you worked there?" Birdie put her purse in her lap. One hand gripped it tight, while the other held her coffee cup.

"A few years."

"That's a long time."

"Yeah." He looked away.

"Two years for me. I'm a clerk."

"A clerk?"

She leaned forward, eyes wide. "It's all papers and words and broken promises."

The wind whistled past the door, punching the door's bell, making it ring. It sounded loud and shrill in the cold weather.

But not in here. Under Birdie's blinking and wide brown eyes, a warmth flooded him. No shivers or chills. No aching in his jaw from clinching his teeth against the frozen temperatures, only coziness.

Birdie reached across the table and placed her hand inches from his hot chocolate.

"Have you thought about doing something else?" She sipped.

Oscar adjusted his slouched position. "Work is work."

"Do you have any hobbies or activities you like to do?"

"Just work."

"Surely, there's more than work. Do you read books?"

Oscar glanced down at his hot chocolate. It bubbled and steamed. Its surface trembled and split open. Oscar's hand shook as the mug opened into a gaping maw, and it seemed to draw all the diner's sounds into its chocolaty depths. The music pounded louder and louder, drowning out the voices of the customers, until the air was thick with its relentless beat.

Oscar leapt from his chair and stumbled back in shock, his fingers numbing. Their tips turned into iced daggers. He rubbed them together, trying desperately to steady himself in the chaos.

Just moments before, he almost took off his hoodie.

But now...

"I, I gotta go." His chair crashed to the floor.

Birdie stood too. Her thin lips moved.

They didn't say anything.

Oscar yanked his hood over his head and backpedaled enough to not collide with the table.

He rushed out into the icy night.

OSCAR RUSHED THROUGH THE SLICK, DARKENED streets. The music had faded, but the cold remained. The frigidness infiltrated him, and now, not only was he frozen outside, but he ached inside. A deep, hollowed-out vacancy in his core, a blackened fireplace with extinguished flames.

Had there ever been a fire inside me?

Warmth like in Birdie's eyes? He spied the roaring flames inside her. It flickered in her eyes.

"Bruh. Hey, bruh. You ain't cold?" One of the men

along the barrel fire shouted at him. He wore a faded and filthy wool hat pulled down low, over his ears and eyebrows.

Oscar slowed.

"Yeah. Young blood, I'm talkin' to you. You cold, ain't you?" He scraped his fingers together, their sound like the crunch of bones. "It's a frozen hell out here. Come o'er here and get thawed out."

Green Hat nodded at the flames. They rose like hungry animals. He threw an armful of trash into the barrel.

Oscar stepped into the men's circle, hunched against the night's icy air. The others' bodies crowded around him, their heat shielding him like a pack of penguins clinging to one another for warmth. He extended his hands over the burning blaze and his fingers thawed, but only a little.

"See? It ain't bad." Green Hat offered a ragged smile, but Oscar noticed the cruel glint in his eyes and heard an acidic note in his tone. He felt the cold down his neck again and knew it was no longer from the chill outside.

"You ain't new 'round here," Green Hat said.

"I—I work at the factory," Oscar replied before he could stop himself, regretting it almost instantly as he heard Baseball Cap's sinister laughter.

"Ah, you a workin' man, huh? More like he's working for the man!" Baseball Cap sneered.

Fear raced through Oscar's veins as he removed his hands from the flames and shoved them into his pockets.

"Oh, don't pay them no 'tention." Green Hat clapped Oscar on the shoulder with rough familiarity. "You belong 'ere." His voice sounded like a jagged blade cutting through the night air. "You one of us. Beacon Homes family."

SUNLIGHT HEATED UP THE CONCRETE AND surrounding brick buildings in Beacon Homes. All that hot pavement created one hell of a pressure cooker. Folks' tempers had been burnt to short and frayed ends. People could fry eggs and meth on the sidewalks. Oscar Banks rounded the curve, nostrils flared, running full out with legs pumping and heart heaving down Magnolia Avenue, through the Beacon's belly. The rec center sat in the community guts. It fed the youth's interest in sports, cards, and relationships.

"Ay, O! Where you goin?" Green Hat shouted as Oscar streaked past.

The pounding rhythm filled Oscar's ears. He glanced in the caller's direction and slowed to a walk. He turned around and headed back to the barrel, blackened and vacant.

Nothing burned.

No flames.

No fire.

Green Hat clasped him on the back and guided Oscar into the huddle of other sweaty and shiny faces, crumbling in hunger, and scarred in poverty.

"You one of us."

Oscar nodded. "Yeah."

"Stop runnin'. You one B Homes. Right?"

Oscar looked around at the others.

"Yeah. I'm B Homes."

AS DARK THE NIGHT

Stella spied the shadows huddled in the corners. Dangerous and cold, they waited in the gloom. Perfect reflections of the overcast morning. Hurt took time, and her failed relationship lingered, along with the pain. It would heal, albeit slow, like an infected wound.

Memories would forever resurface, because they always did. Some people preferred to be on their own, and she counted herself among them. Now. She thought he'd be great. Senior. Basketball player. Love of anime. As she drank her coffee, images crept into her head, with long spider-like legs carrying their webbing of memories and emotions, tethering them to her brain.

A cruel laugh escaped her. She caught herself, but her anger flared.

Why shouldn't she laugh? Didn't she deserve to after it ended?

When you battle evil, you get burned. Stella's burns festered inside her. They bled and puked out hideous green infection that soured her ability to hope, poisoned her optimism, and leeched misery into her daily life.

The shadows flickered across her shut blinds. They winked across the room in secretive moves, as if waiting for something. They had always been there, looming with shimmering darkness. Since puberty hit, they had lurked in dimly lit corners, remaining her constant companions, as if being seventeen didn't come with enough baggage.

When she finished her drink, she placed her spoon and mug in the sink and turned to face her living space. Furry Fantastic: a black tabby who looked like the sun sprayed out of him as he sunned himself along the living room's bay windows, twitched when she clicked her tongue.

"Some of us have the life." He meowed in agreement.

Stella's cell phone rang. Her fingers throbbed from gripping the sink behind her. Centuries passed before glorious silence returned. Stella swallowed a hard knot of anxiety.

When spots dotted her vision, she forced herself to take a breath.

"Let us set you free. You are in so much pain," the whispered voices spoke in unison.

Stella shut her eyes to the wilted plants; discarded delivery food containers; and garbage bags, tied and waiting to be taken to the dumpster. Maybe the shadows were right. She should give in and give up. Let their tendrils creep into her skull and finger her brain. This interference caused sharp headaches and nausea, Rendering her bedridden for weeks at a time.

Medication had failed. Prayer had failed.

She had failed.

The shadows rippled like water, as if silently laughing. One of the elongated lines stretched farther and then stood. It grew taller, wider. Stella tried to back up farther, but she was already pressed against the sink, her heart hammering at the intrusion. This shaft of shadows broke free of the others, cackling softly as it did so,

It formed a face that split into deep yellow eyes and a jagged slash mouth. The head continued to shift and mold itself, becoming a skull with round eye sockets filled with small glowing lights.

Was this some dark, frightening, and awful message from her depression?

"I am Wren." The inky shadow produced a hand with long fingers.

Its other side clutched what appeared to be a book. The yellowing flesh emerged and the full person—if you could call it that—emerged from the shadow's cloak.

Fear flooded Stella's mouth, making her ill. It chased away the coffee's sweetness. Her momma's words returned: *You're wasting the day. A day the good Lord Jesus gave. A gift from God.* Literally.

But Stella didn't have the strength to move. The life leeched from the room, leaving behind bleak, washed-out colors. Pulsating fear pumped through her. It hardened into a pit in her belly. It blocked how much she could eat, so her appetite faded to nothing.

Stella understood that sophisticated spirits lived. Her momma and grandmamma were dyed-in-the-wool Pentecostals who spoke in tongues. Those holy spirits visited the church, not in her home. Not really. Shadows. Nothing more. They didn't insinuate themselves into people's lives.

"You're always watching me. I feel you watching," Stella whispered as her throat closed over the knot of fear.

Wren grinned—showing black teeth. "There are spirits all around you. I watch to learn."

"You watch to mimic."

"I have watched the light die in many others." Wren

reached for her, stopped just short of touching Stella's shoulder. "Being human does not interest me."

"You see us as what? Entertainment? What are we to you? Tools?"

Wren shrugged.

"If only they did not keep breaking..."

"You shouldn't be so rough!" it screeched. Once it regained its composure, it said, "Not to worry. I do not kill what I already have. And you, dear, are wrapped up tight."

In its arrogance, it revealed its true purpose.

A good blow to the nose would remind it that it didn't have her all wrapped up, but Wren didn't have one. The empty cavern where its sinuses would've been, had it been a person, looked like dark shapes on a map. It had managed to form hair. Its halo of gray tufts held sharp edges. No doubt it remained upright and breathing by venom and fury. It reeked of old vomit and stale piss.

"What do you want?" Stella clutched the sleeves of her Bulldog sweatshirt over her hands. The real terror, the real pain, was the presence of this strange evil. Perhaps it had always been there, in the shadows, lurking, and learning her tender spots to torment.

"You still miss him? He, who was loose with his lies and tight with his attention?" Wren's matter-of-fact tone chilled her.

Stella closed her eyes, then opened them again. Despite her wishes, Wren remained.

"You're in such agonizing pain," Wren whispered. Its breath smelled of rot, hot against her cheek.

The atmosphere in the kitchen felt thick enough to touch.

"Leave. Me. Alone." Stella knocked its hand away from her face.

Wren pouted. "Give me a chance to display my talents."

"Does it even matter?"

"There's nothing to worry about. You'll continue to feel nothing, and I, well, I get to feed on your delicious despair. I hunger, Stella."

Wren's greasy voice made her skin crawl. It feasted on her depression, on her pain. It wanted her to be like it was, numb and empty. Bile pushed against her throat. Faint and dizzy, she wiped her face, and her hand came away wet. Tears.

Wren's cold glare didn't waver. Looming so close to her now, its lipless mouth twitched at the corners as if that void-within-a-void had a mind of its own. Even now, Wren drank sips of her sorrow, making her world spin. As it did so, its shape became more defined, more filled in.

"You haven't slept in weeks," Wren cajoled.

Stella's patience waned. "Stop littering my life!"

Wren bristled. Its yellow eyes flashed. A wet, stabbing sound filled the room as its approximation of an index finger touched her temple.

"You will give to me, all of yourself! It's a slow process. 'Tis true, but you will give in, bit by bit. One day, you will find yourself unable to crawl out of bed, unable to make your own decisions. I will devour those pieces of you until you see me. Fully." Wren levitated as it clapped its hands in joy.

I'm already there! Stella thought.

The shadows had always been there: in her crib, in her bedroom, in her classrooms.

They'd watched her cry; seen her cut, scarlet blood welling; been riveted by her pain. They witnessed the agony she faced for simply existing. Wren and its kind had been feasting on her the whole time.

Even as she wept, it increased her suffering, eating every chunk of her mental disease with glee.

Why couldn't it show some damn humanity? Because it wasn't human.

At this, Furry Fantastic leapt onto the counter and shrieked at Wren. All fur raised in alarm and tail straight in warning. Furry appeared to be glowing.

Wren's eyes became saucers, and it hissed in return.

"You cannot be here." Stella shook her head to clear the cotton haze. She doubted the thing that called itself Wren had grown a consciousness as hastily as it had grown its imitation body parts. It understood her. It had for a long time. So she spoke to it again now: "You. Are. Not. Welcome here."

Furry Fantastic pounced at Wren. It cowered and vanished just as Furry's claws sliced through the air.

Hazy and hot, Stella pushed her sleeves up to her elbows. Surely the air conditioner had kicked on, so why the clammy sweat? Two warring sections of her body unfurled: hot and cold.

"Thank you, Fur." She scooped him up into her arms. He purred out his welcome.

<hr>

LATER THAT AFTERNOON, STELLA LAY ON THE SOFA —her surrogate bed most of the day.

She didn't have the strength or desire to do much of anything. Once the TV came on, Furry Fantastic leapt down from his usual sunspot and walked over to her. Stella tossed the blanket over her legs, cuddled against the sofa's thick pillows, and hunkered down to merge with nothingness.

The doorbell rang. Furry meowed at the intrusion.

"I know. I keep myself to myself, so why are folks bothering me today?" Stella petted him and tugged the blanket up to her chin. She inched closer to the sofa's seam, to the velvety dark. "If we ignore them, they'll move on."

The intruders leaned on the bell. Annoyed, Furry Fantastic hopped down, roaring his protests as he headed toward the kitchen.

What could be so important? With her eyes burning, Stella got up, too. She went to the door and spied through the keyhole. Her momma always warned her to check before opening a door.

Two people stood outside her door. A woman, on the left, was blonde, but skinny and in need of a wash. The man on the right had beautiful eyes. Empty eyes. She could see that because this one stared directly into the keyhole. The male was also in need of a good scrubbing. Common voices, faded unicorn hair, and ragged clothing all spoke to danger. Both bodies as white as china dolls.

"Aye, they left you a package. The mail dude," the male said.

Sweat broke out across Stella's body. A package? Outside held all kinds of dangers, namely people. They sucked. They hated. They participated in dissolving whatever good will Stella had left. She wiped her damp hands on her pants.

"Go on! Get cracking somewhere else!"

Stella's affliction had manifested as weakness. These creatures milling about her front door could only make a dire situation worse. Neighbors. Nosy ones, too. Once someone is afflicted, they know it.

They felt it. Although she normally kept busy, a moving target was still a target.

There were things in the world people couldn't see, but no one could train them for that or the perils those unseen forces brought with them.

Not waiting to see the people on the porch leave, Stella started toward her sofa. The doorbell's ringing continued.

This time it was followed by shouts. "It's still out here!"

With a huff of annoyance, she turned back to the keyhole. They switched to pounding on the door. Stella closed her eyes. Her world shifted and she took leave of her body. Sailing above her dark-stained wood floor, she slipped through the ceiling, then the roof, and peered below to the visitors outside on her porch. An awfulness washed over her. The people at her door now wore professional dress. Black suits and crisp white shirts. Polished shoes and tidy hair. The man menacing her grinned at the keyhole.

"Dontaye sends his love." The man lifted his hand and waved.

Beside him, the woman tilted her head to the side. "He misses you. He wants you."

What the hell?

Agony exploded inside of her. Stella screamed and when her eyes flapped open, she found herself back on the sofa.

Standing at the foot of it, Wren snapped its fingers. "Stella?"

Stella bolted upright.

"It is amazing how weak humans are when faced with the supernatural…" Static crackled across her TV and drowned out Wren's words.

"Get out of here!" Stella's head lolled to the side. A fluttering had taken up residence in her belly.

"Stella." It didn't say more.

"There's somewhere I need to be." If it wouldn't leave, she would. She pushed herself to stand on wobbly legs. She could go to the park.

Wren reached out a hand to bar her path. "I'm not here to hurt you."

The moment it said those words, Stella knew. Of course, Wren meant to hurt her. How else would it be able to continue to drink the dark thoughts of her depression? She knew its kind well. Once she stepped out into the light, the people had disappeared.

"Let me pass." Stella avoided eye contact.

For all the brilliant sunlight outside, darkness huddled inside. It had been that way since middle school and high school was no different. The sun's illumination failed to breach her space. It stopped short, as if fearful of being consumed.

"Do you not want to be free of the hurt? The burning anger?" Wren spread its hands wide. "I thirst."

Stella's heart banged against her chest. Sweat rolled down her face. The hairs on her arms and along her neck stood at attention. A nervous mix burrowed into her belly, making her nauseous.

"I'm sweet tempered." Wren's high-pitched cackling made her shudder.

"You're not the first to come here." Stella seethed.

Greedy bastards. They siphoned off her joy. They plunged their knives into her emotions and twisted until her sorrow and pain poured out like a fountain. They took long drinks that drained her, so she constantly ached. "Go back into hiding."

She looked over her shoulder in time to see Wren scowl as Furry Fantastic zoomed in from the kitchen. Wren dissolved once more.

"Thank you." Stella sighed, wiping her brow.

FURRY FANTASTIC'S EMERALD EYES CLOSED AS IF pondering the situation. Stella's safe space infiltrated by the very thing she sought to escape. Those emotional pieces remained scattered at her feet. Did she dare reach down to reclaim the sharp fragments? Even if she put them together, they'd never be whole. Not really. Fissures and fault cracks would remain.

Furry Fantastic brushed her ankle before going off to prowl around the rest of the townhouse. The time read a little after two in the afternoon. The shadows remained still, but Stella couldn't keep her eyes open any longer. She couldn't shake the feeling that it had all gone wrong with Wren. Nestled once more between the emptiness and blanket warmth, she slept.

Fur's constant crying and sharp-nailed kneading forced Stella off the couch. Time to get up. If she could. Clawing out of the emotional quagmire made her body sing with fatigue.

Big green eyes looked down at her. "Meow."

"When are you not hungry?" Stella scratched behind his ear. "Come on." She got out of bed. "You let me have an hour." She sounded cranky, even to herself.

A single stroke, a thousand deaths began today. Stella could almost hear Furry Fantastic utter those words as a worn fluffy warrior. As the whirling of the can opener broke the quiet, Stella noted how all the cans' screams sounded the same. Stella hadn't slept well, but sleep didn't matter. Whenever she rested her head, the rollercoaster raged on, snatching her inner shrieks from her while buried in sleep's rigid embrace.

Her cell phone rang.

"Let's go to a late lunch," Marcia sang as soon as Stella said hello.

Marcia had been her best friend since elementary school, and she'd just gotten a new car.

"I'm busy," Stella mumbled into the phone, already regretting not letting the call roll to voicemail.

"No, you ain't," Marcia declared before Stella finished talking. "I want steak and I don't want to eat alone."

"I'm not hungry."

"I am. Come on. You need sunlight," Marcia prodded. "Stella..."

"I'll be there in ten."

Stella groaned. Now she had to shower, put on clothes, and a hat.

There wasn't enough energy to even consider doing her hair.

Before she changed her mind, she willed herself to the wash. Step one. Step two. *The body was a canvas. Nourish it with love*, her late momma used to say.

The water pounded her flesh. Her mood remained numb, even after lathering and rinsing. In all the commercials, the people were cheery once clean—grinning and skinny in their white towels and decorated showers.

Time crept by in a heavy haze of dressing, teeth brushing, and face washing. Something about her townhouse made her safe. By the time Marcia arrived on her doorstep, the downpour had ceased. The juxtaposition of quick time and slow time left Stella out of sorts. She didn't move in step with herself, almost like she viewed herself from a short distance away.

"Yay!" Marcia hugged her, tugging Stella into the crushing embrace. Dark jeans, heels, and her roseate blouse were beautiful. Her long dreads had been confined in a bun. Makeup applied with rigid precision.

They climbed into Marcia's two-seater and Stella floated along, flapping in the wind. She was both there and not there. Wavering between the void of numbness and the iciness of anxiety, Stella listened as Marcia talked about her Instagram and who was going out with who. Stella did a lot of nodding.

"...So, how's Furry Fantastic?" Marcia glanced at her as she made a left on Maple.

"Fine." Stella shrugged.

Marcia gave her side-eyed warning.

"Fluffy," Stella added.

Marcia laughed. "He obviously isn't a great conversationalist. You're practically mute."

"Well, he's a cat, so..." Stella shifted in her seat. Marcia roared with laughter.

They stopped talking as Marcia drove on. Stella slid outside herself once more.

The landscape bled by in a gray fog. Beside her, Marcia bounced to her own rhythm. They arrived at Joey's Diner. Marcia pulled into an open spot just inside the parking garage and shifted into park. She dropped her hands in her lap, turned to Stella, and said, "It is good to see you. You been hiding."

"It's hot." Stella held Marcia's sad gaze.

"You thinking about dating? I heard Curtis has a crush…"

"No…"

"…he told Tamara he wanted you." Marcia's magnetic personality pushed on.

"Full stop." Stella held up her hand. *God, let something ward off the approaching platitudes and positive memes*, she prayed.

"Just worried about you." Marcia dropped the intense staring and plopped back against the driver's seat. "That ish with Dontaye was foul."

"I'm fine." Stella's voice rose to fake level cheer—along the lines of reality television personalities.

"No, you're not. I know you. Look at me, 'Ella. I know you ain't you. You ain't been you for a minute."

Stella sighed. If only she could explain it in words.

"Let's go eat." She pushed the door open without waiting for Marcia to play shrink. The sooner she got started, the sooner it would end. She longed for the warm blanket cocoon of the sofa and Furry's low rumbling warmth nestled beside her. She missed her safety.

Out here, in the urban world, Stella lacked protection.

Others' unrestrained wills and unchecked privilege rained down on her. Exposed, Stella hurried into Joey's.

God, couldn't this be over soon?

Marcia called after her and, once she reached Stella, she grabbed her shoulder. "'Ella!"

Stella tried to brush her off. "Let it go."

Something in her face must have warned Marcia, because she dropped her hand.

"Yeah. Okay. Come on."

The lunch crowd in Joey's buzzed. Marcia navigated the tables until she found available seating at one of the booths. Folks piled up at the counter and filled out the tables. Stella eased down into the booth's crinkling seat and tried to count the moments until this torment would end.

Once the food arrived, Stella stopped gripping the table's edge. With aching knuckles, she picked up her spoon. Marcia had been talking, but she hadn't really been listening.

"Yours smells wonderful but looks awful." Marcia quirked an eyebrow at the bowl of orange liquid in front of Stella. The sprinkle of nutmeg stood out against the color.

"Butternut squash soup." Stella stirred the thick liquid, swirling in the nutmeg. "It's tastier than it looks."

"Hope so." Marcia cut into her steak.

All around them flavors wafted in and faded, mixed and mingled with Marcia's perfume. Stella's stomach trembled. The occasional crash from a rogue glass's demise punched through the din. A breath of quiet followed before life erupted again. Stella inhaled the soup's rich aroma to steady herself. On either side of the booth, animated people lunched and laughed, talked, and tore through their meals with a passion Stella lacked. She sighed as she took in their happiness.

Marcia said, "How come you don't come out? Leo's party last Saturday…"

Stella shrugged. "I like being home."

"It's a cage of lights and rules!"

A cage. Stella nodded. "The great thing about cages—no one gets in either."

Silence stretched out in concert with time. A quiet center in a whirlwind of conversations, their booth remained in its tight bubble. Marcia had moved to the small side salad —when she broke their silence.

"I love you, girl. I wanna help." Marcia looked across the table at her, concerned.

"There's nothing you can do."

"But what is it?"

Stella shrugged. "I dunno. That's why you can't help. I know you want to do something. That'll make *you* feel better."

"*Me* feel better?" Marcia sat back in her chair. A frown changed her face. "What's that supposed to mean?"

The annoyance rolled forward in Stella. "Like this. Inviting me to lunch makes you feel better about how great your life is going. Or maybe it eases that secret guilt because you think I deserve what happened."

"What do you hear in your head? I want to see you happy. Hell, I want you to be alive."

Stella's cheeks burned, and she folded her arms, abandoning all pretense of eating. "Happiness is an illusion."

"We're all doing our best. Sometimes we fly." Marcia smiled. "You need to soar."

"My wings have been clipped," Stella retorted.

"Yeah, so grow them back."

"It takes time." Stella looked up at Marcia. "And, with all broken things, the healing hurts."

Marcia's budding smile faltered. "I see."

Stella doubted it, but she kept it to herself. They'd already drawn strange looks and hard whispers from the other diners. The illness spilled into her belly again. Marcia tried to get her out to socialize, and Stella ruined it. The level of pity in Marcia's face made her feel worse.

"Excuse me." Stella scooted out of the booth.

Marcia tossed her napkin onto her plate and inched out of the booth. She hugged Stella. As she held her close, Marcia whispered, "I know you're hurting, and that hurts me."

Stella hugged her back. "I'm sorry."

"Not your fault." Marcia released her, turned, and started collecting her receipt to pay the cashier.

Once they exited, Marcia continued. "Look. Don't keep shutting the door. One day, when you go to open it, no one will be there. So, get your head sorted."

"I hear you."

They returned to the car. Normally, Marcia's bubbly self would lift her up, too.

Not today. Marcia's usual fierce personality had been extinguished. Stella sunk lower. Her sickness remained infectious. This was why she didn't leave her home. She'd contaminated her best friend. Who knew what Marcia would do to heal herself?

"What's your plan?" Marcia backed out of the parking space but cut a glance at Stella as she did so.

Plan? Today hadn't gone as planned. Things rarely did, so why bother?

Didn't the last five months prove that?

"You can't stay like this."

"I need time."

"It heals all wounds," Marcia said. "School starts back in like six weeks."

"Right." Stella watched the neighborhood emerge as they left the parking garage's cover.

The rain-drenched day rattled on. Detached. Withdrawn, they continued in silence. Thick, heavy traffic clogged the lanes. Frequent scarlet lights illuminated the gray as folks struggled to navigate the soaked streets. The wind whistled as it whipped rain against the sports car; lashing out as if angered that humans had dared.

How could she explain to Marcia that each day felt as if she'd woken up in her own coffin?

Marcia pulled alongside the cars parked near the townhouse. Stella opened the passenger door. "Bye."

"Talk to me!" Marcia put the car into park, but Stella waved goodbye. She restrained the urge to race into her home.

Thunder rumbled overhead. Fleeing the forthcoming downpour, Stella hurried and unlocked the door. She breathed a sigh of relief and stepped into the waiting arms of solitude. The closed door brought with it—comfort. Relief. The box of Furry's cat food remained outside the door.

Damp. Tired. Stella breathed deeply as the roll of anxiety lulled. Just then, out of the corner of her eye, she saw the shadows flicker.

Eager to seek her out, they shimmered. Seeing Marcia

had caused her an emotional explosion, and it had drained her. The darkness gnawed at her. Each inch of her ached.

IN MINUTES, SHE'D STRIPPED HER CLOTHES AND gotten into bed. The covers glided over her, and she snuggled farther beneath. The bed welcomed her with soft quiet. No questions. No requirements. She cuddled against the nothing. Wrapped her arms around the vacancy in her bed and closed her eyes to await the dark.

Stella didn't enjoy it—the dark. Almost as if on cue, Furry Fantastic leapt onto the bed. The cat seemed to know when the hole inside her became too great. He walked into the giant place beside Stella, kneading and nesting the space. He circled it before cuddling beside her. His rumbling soothed her. The darkness's fingers reached out and enveloped her heart, spreading that numbing ache.

Yet when Furry lay beside her, his warmth pushed back the hollow cold.

But only for a moment.

Only for one fleeting moment.

"You're in such pain, delicious agonizing pain," Wren whispered, its breath rotting and hot against her cheek.

Stunned, Stella bolted upright, arms flailing. The scream dying just as she awoke.

Why was Wren breathing? It wasn't alive—right?

The atmosphere in her bedroom felt thick enough to touch. Didn't it hear her before? Emboldened by some other world, it continued to breach the security of her home, her sanctuary. The devious shadows had come to collect—again.

Stella fell back onto her pillow. A flicker materialized beside her bed.

"Go home to your mother," Stella croaked.

"I have no mother," Wren said with a cackle.

"Let me refresh your memory. Leave. Me. Alone." Stella knocked its hand away from her face.

Wren pouted; slashes of flesh pushed forward in some facial expression. "Give me a chance to display my talents."

"You Seekers are all the same. Moths to flames, ready to burn." Stella pushed herself back against the bed's headboard. Her grand had told her all about them, but she'd never actually met one.

"You know there's nothing to worry about." Bile pushed against her throat, and she swallowed it down.

Feeling faint and dizzy, Stella wiped her face. Her hand came away wet. She'd muddled through the last string of days, all tethered together by a sticky film of tears and fury. She couldn't keep going like this. Marica's words came back to her.

Wren's cold, darting glare didn't waver as it stood at the end of her bed. It was quite keen to drink her misery. Its lipless mouth twitched at the corners. Even now, it drank sips of her, tiny gulps of her sorrow, making her world spin. As it did so, it became more defined, more filled in.

Wren bristled. The yellow of its eyes flashed. A wet, stabbing sound filled the room.

Plunged into the void of her bleached-out life, Stella clutched her pillow to her chest against the auditory assault. *Don't give in. Don't give up.*

"I will devour those pieces of you until you see me. Fully."

Stella bit her lip to keep from lashing out that she was already there. Her tortured mind pounded in pain, and she winced as she turned away, knowing they'd done this before, said this before. Wren could increase her suffering, eating every chunk of her disease with glee.

Why couldn't he show some damn humanity?

Because it/he/they wasn't/weren't human.

Do you want to die?

The question bulldozed into her mind. She flinched because it wasn't a voice she'd heard before. She looked down in her lap to see Furry Fantastic glaring at her, his green eyes wide as if concentrating on something.

Do you want to die?

No.

Then fight this damn thing. FIGHT with all you have against the dark! The Shadows!

I... I am so tired.

You aren't alone. We will fight together.

"Furry?" Stella frowned at him. "That's you. Isn't it? In my head?"

Furry meowed and turned away. His hair stood on end, and he hissed at Wren.

Furry was right. She refused to crumble, to fold. No way would she give herself over to the shadows.

"Allow me in, Stella. I do not refuse an invitation." Wren tapped its fingers together.

Wheezing, she swung her legs over the edge of the bed. As she pushed herself to stand, the rattling wheeze sounded loud in the bedroom. Her lips trembled. Wren winked before her. So close—it didn't move, but it didn't come closer either.

Furry stood between them.

"Stop touching me." Her strained, weak voice made her pause from saying more.

A tightness in her chest made breathing difficult. She stumbled over something dark.

"I can come in now, or I can come in later, which you won't like, Stella." Wren tapped its fingers together again, a maddening repetition.

Furry Fantastic meowed. With an unflinching glare, he bared his teeth and kept hissing. Her furball of hisses rounded on Wren with tail high and claws at the ready. Furry Fantastic howled in fury, swiping at the shadowy visitor. Wren's features sharpened. Its eyes narrowed, and its non-existent nose disappeared into the folds of its thin skin, almost melting like ice cream in the summer.

"Call your beast off!" it demanded.

"No! Don't come here again. We will devour you!" Stella balled her hands into fists.

Furry leapt at Wren, claws out, hissing all the way.

Wren shrieked and folded itself into the gloominess, winking out in an instant.

Stella scooped a now-purring Furry Fantastic into her arms. As she stroked his fur, light emitted from him, crawled up Stella's arms, and outward into the bedroom.

Everything brightened. She could breathe again. She sat down on the bed, cradling the cat in her arms. Tears streamed down her cheeks.

"Thank you," she whispered.

You're welcome. I'm hungry.

"Great. Momma's home." Stella kissed Furry's head.

THE TELL-TALE TATTOO

"Start again from the beginning, Officer Bloom."

Detective Trevor Bell pushed his fists into his pants' pockets. His melodious voice resounded in the tight room. He glanced out the window to the rain falling in buckets on Nashville's drab and dreary streets. The interview space reeked of tense sweat. The overhead fluorescent lights poured down harsh yellowing light.

Hunched against the worn and wobbly table, Officer Gary Bloom glared at the blank paper and pen in front of him. Dressed in civilian clothes, a t-shirt sporting the Blue Lives Matter flag, and jeans, he scowled at Detective Krista Fox seated across from him.

"I've already told you three times. It ain't gonna change, Krista." Gary ran a hand across his buzz-cut hair. He crossed his arms and cocked his head. "Can I go now?"

"It's *Detective* Fox, and we need answers, *Officer* Bloom." He shot forward in his seat, but she didn't flinch and she held his eye contact. "A man is dead."

"And the media has made it a circus," Detective Bell chimed in. "We have some conflicting accounts of what happened, so we're asking witnesses to help flesh things out."

Gary scratched at his neck and tugged on the t-shirt's flat

collar. "All right. Fine. On Saturday, I worked the march in downtown Nashville. I'm there, in full riot gear, sweating my balls off, to make sure people's right to protest is protected."

"That's our job, officer." Detective Fox wrote something in her black leather-bound notebook.

GARY HISSED OUT HIS FRUSTRATION. *THESE TWO desk jockeys don't know the first thing about policing. They got their degrees and walked into detective jobs.*

A sharp flash of pain forced his teeth to clench, and he sat ramrod straight in the chair.

What the hell was that?

Gary gently touched the area around his neck. His fingers came away wet, with blood on them.

Probably an insect bite. God knows what's crawling around in here.

It hurt more than any other insect bite he'd ever had. He breathed through the pain and glared at the detective.

"Look, all I'm saying is the place was a powder keg waiting to happen. It was like lighting a firecracker—the whole damn pack! Boom!"

Thunder growled outside the windows, and electricity crackled in the worn and weary room.

"Go on." Detective Bell came away from the window and stood to the right of Detective Fox.

Now the detective is gonna turn up the heat on me. Loser. I'm a pro at interrogation.

"It was a tense and dangerous scene. When you got that

kinda mix..." Gary swallowed the ache in his throat. An image sliced through his mind.

A Black woman cradled a man in her arms. Her dark eyes narrowed in mournful anger at Gary. Those eyes burrowed into him, a thousand little daggers, and he reeled backward, stumbling to his feet, to flee. He threw the branch aside. She stroked the man's garish and hideous neck tattoo, the kind all filthy gang members and thugs had. It spelled out something in Old English script, but blood from the wound obscured some of the letters. The first one was an M.

"Officer?" Detective Fox rapped on the table. "Officer Bloom?"

"Yeah?" Gary startled in the wooden seat.

What's this? His fingers traced the raised swatch of skin. It burned like fire. He sucked in a steadying breath and released it slowly.

"You were speaking about the protest scene..."

"Uh, right. I mean, the scene speaks for itself." Gary splayed his hands wide, as if he had nothing else to add.

Detective Fox scratched out several more notes on her pad.

"Tell us about the fight," Detective Bell said, breaking the ensuing quiet.

Gary closed his eyes as the mob's roar exploded, wrenching him back to the memory, to the place.

No justice! No peace! No justice! No peace!

"I dunno anything about the damn fight. I dunno who started it, but it was probably some loud-mouth loser..."

"You're a trained police officer. Can you be more specific? Height? Hair color? Clothing? Ethnicity?" Detective Fox looked up from her notepad. "Anything?"

Gary closed his eyes and clenched his fists beneath the table.

"We're confident in the case we're building." Detective Bell licked his lips. "As I said before, we're collecting additional statements."

"All I know is it's peaceful one second and the next it's quick explosions of violence like the Fourth of July." Gary wiped the thin, runny blood on his pants. Couldn't they see him bleeding?

I need to get out of here. I might've gotten bit by a recluse spider.

Gary slid his hand up to his neck and placed it over the searing and weepy flesh.

His finger traced what felt like the raised, ornate curves of an Old-English letter M. Chills skated up his spine. But he must be imagining it. Damn interrogation tactics. They were getting to him after all. He coughed to clear his throat and his head.

"Is there anything else? Can I go?"

Detective Fox's arched eyebrows rose higher. "Why are you so upset? We're trying to get to the truth."

The skin on his neck flared in burning irritation. He slapped it and then rubbed it with the tips of his fingers. It felt like a sunburn.

"You know what, *Detective*? I'm not mad. I'm *pissed!* Why? Let me tell you. I stood among my comrades in arms, in the blazing heat. Hell, even the sun was angry. The weekend means relaxation. People should be grateful for what they get, you know? I mean, they already get welfare, scholarships, and affirmative action. If the lot of them weren't a bunch of damn criminals, my brothers would be alive and enjoying their weekend instead of rotting in coffins because of those damn crybabies. What about us? It's not safe out here for cops, and these damn people are angry because we gotta protect ourselves. I wanted to be home, under the A/C with a beer in my hand and the game on TV. But I wasn't. I did my job."

"A person is dead, *Officer* Bloom." Detective Fox shot a glance at her fellow detective. "We are only trying to get to the truth and catch a killer."

"Sure."

Gary slouched down in the chair. He massaged his neck and sighed in a noisy manner.

"We've talked to other officers as well as participants. Today we're talking to you." Detective Bell flipped open a manila folder on the table. He took out a 4X6 photograph and pushed it toward the policeman. "We pulled this image from surveillance cameras in the area. This is activist Lorenzo Alfonso Rodriguez, age 23. He died yesterday."

Gary hitched his chin higher. "I know."

Detective Bell continued, as if Gary hadn't spoken. "His wallet, phone and jewelry were missing, but we were able to identify him from his fingerprints..."

"Immigration, right?"

"Colorado. Born and raised," Detective Fox countered, unsmiling. Her tone betrayed her disgust.

Gary leered at her. *Women. What do they know?*

A searing heat flared along his neck, and he slapped his hand over it. *Damn it!*

His fingers traced the raised mark, sloping into the next set of punished flesh. He swallowed as a trickle of cold sweat raced down his face. *What the hell is this? What's happen-*

ing? Is it some kinda disease? His stomach clenched into a ball of tight fear, twisting in terror.

"Lorenzo was struck in the throat and head by a tree branch." Detective Bell tapped the picture. "His wounds were too severe for the doctors to save him."

The air conditioning rattled, like a dry throat sputtering for words as its life force poured out of it.

"You know when the police close in, suspects will discard evidence," Gary said.

Why did I bring up evidence? Did they notice? Gawd. Do they suspect me?

The branch had been a weapon of opportunity.

Gary glanced up from the table at Detective Fox. Her eyes, dark brown, narrowed in suspicion and outright revulsion, like the Black woman at the march. He knew this point in the investigation was when the detective would pressure the suspect—him.

"Are you okay?" Detective Bell removed his suit jacket.

Gary stiffened and shifted his gaze to the man. "Yeah. Why?"

"You keep scratching your neck."

"Mosquito bite."

It feels a bit long to be a bite. Probably more than one. Those winged bastards were out in full force. Just like those annoying ass protestors.

The detective leaned forward on the chair's back.

Gary mopped his face with his hand. "It's hot in here. You tryin' to sweat me?"

"What?" Detective Bell peered at him. "You can't be serious? The A/C's on."

"I need a break." Gary pushed his chair back so hard it banged against the floor.

He didn't bother picking it up.

"Officer!" Detective Fox called after him.

He stalked out of the interview (*interrogation*) room and down the hall, directly into the men's restroom. During police questioning, he would deny everything if they tried to pin anything on him.

The lights flickered as he entered and marched to the sink. He gripped the rounded porcelain edges and glared at the mirror.

And shrieked. "What the hell?"

In bold, Old English script, a palm-size *M* blared from his neck, in the area below his ear. The snarled swoop and cursive letter reached across to a lowercase angry black *u*. The inky raised line snaked to the neighboring *r*. He read the rest of the letters and the wretched word they spelled—backward in the mirror, but clear to him and God and anyone. Gary wheezed as he held on to the sink to keep from dropping to the floor. His pale skin hummed in scarlet, inflamed flesh as if he'd gotten a new tattoo. It felt hot, worse than a sunburn now, raw and abraded.

With his throat dry, he gouged at the letters, trying to scratch them out of existence. He tore at his skin, his nails coming out crimson. The agony didn't stop him. He twisted his head and looked again, his heart hammering like a freight train in his chest. The tattoo remained black and angry against his flushed flesh. Gary watched his Adam's apple bob in terror.

Gary traced the tattoo. The raised cursive remained.

He didn't daydream or hallucinate, ever. He wasn't now.

He spun around from the mirror. *Did they see it? Did everyone see it?*

Gary searched the bathroom and found nothing to assist him. He snatched several paper towels and stuffed them under the flat collar. He positioned them to cover the tattoo's blackened stretch across the left half of his neck.

It stung as if he'd received a new tattoo only moments ago. A thousand tiny needle pricks' stabbing afterburn. He shut his eyes against the word etched out forever onto his person. With a trembling hand, Gary pushed open the door and slipped out of the restroom.

No way could he go back into that interrogation room. *Do they know?*

THOSE THUGS AND CRIMINALS COULD'VE BEEN carrying a gun or a knife. They didn't care about people's lives. A bunch of vermin.

Gary hunched against the exposure as he hurried down the hallway toward the parking lot outside the station. Those educated morons wouldn't understand the danger ghettos and crack-addicted havens held for good police officers like him.

"Officer Bloom?" Detective Fox met him at the double-door exit. She held a travel mug in her hand and wore a confused expression on her face. "Are you going out for a smoke?"

"I don't smoke," Gary responded without thinking.

"You're heading back to the interview room, then?" She sipped and glanced up at him.

She didn't move out of his way.

Women. So damn bossy.

"Yeah, sure." Gary walked backward and then turned around.

"What happened to your neck?" Detective Fox pointed with her little finger. "Looks like you've scratched yourself something fierce."

Gary froze as a shudder rocketed through him.

Can she see it? Did the towels slip?

With a trembling hand, he reached up and began flattening the paper against his searing skin.

"I, I, uh, scratched the bite into an injury." He offered a weak smile.

Detective Fox didn't have her partner's poker face. "Sure."

With her at his back, Gary was guided to the interview room, where he found Detective Bell placing more photos onto the scarred table. He didn't look up when Gary and his partner entered.

"Okay, take a look at these pictures…" Detective Bell said.

"I don't wanna look at any more photos. I was there, man." Gary folded his arms.

"Sit down, Officer," Detective Fox said as she took the seat across from him once more. "We're going to be a little bit longer, so please, sit."

Play along. The sooner they're satisfied, the sooner you can go home.

Gary sank onto the wooden chair.

"We know you were there, and that's why we want you to look at these images." Detective Bell remained standing, and he tapped on the first one. "This is another one of Lorenzo before the attack."

He placed the photo in front of Gary.

"He was a landscaper. Had a popular business." Detective Fox took out her notepad.

"See here. You're part of the scenery here," Detective Bell pointed at the background spec. "That's you. Right?"

"This was a rage homicide." Detective Fox watched him. "Did you see anyone upset or mad?"

"They were all mad at the march. I told you." Gary leaned his head over to the left, to hide the dark mess on his neck.

"One of the witnesses said the attacker was a cop." Detective Bell brought Gary's attention to him. "When there's a rogue police officer, a murderer with a badge, there's a monster among us. That has to be vanquished."

Monster? He can't possibly mean me. I did that punk a favor.

"There's no boogieman, only whiny people who don't like consequences." Gary's fingers inched up to the pulsating script.

The detectives exchanged a look, and Gary saw it.

They know! They know! I wanna crawl into myself. They can see it!

"Hush! Shush!" Gary shouted.

Detective Fox reared back. Confusion ruined her delicate features for a moment. "What?"

Gary eased to a standing position. "I panicked. Okay? I hit him! The branch, uh, must've crushed his throat, but I didn't mean..."

But that was a lie. He *did* mean...

"Officer Bloom!" Detective Fox stood up. "Calm yourself..."

"I know you can see it. Everyone can see it!" Gary snatched the paper towels and tossed them in the air. They fell like crumpled confetti.

The detectives frowned.

"Gary..." Detective Bell had his hand on the butt of his weapon.

"It's *his* horrid tattoo! *His!* Not mine!"

"Officer Bloom, please!" Detective Fox glanced over at her partner.

"They fucking deserved it! Ungrateful illegals!" Gary sprayed spittle and despair as he collapsed to the floor, still shouting, even as he felt his arms forced behind his back, shouting as the handcuffs went on, shouting as he was led away.

SHEPHERDS
OF THE STORM

The stream of protestors flowed on by, sneakered and booted feet crunching the cracking pavement beneath their weight. A few reporters wore their press identifications on their chests, like targets, separating themselves from the throng. Scores of people marched by Kenika, some with fists high, others with posters, but all shouting truths. *Black Lives Matter! Women's Rights Now! Trans Rights are Human Rights!* punctured the once calm Saturday afternoon. A young woman holding a sign stopped in front of her, as if she meant to press the sign into Kenika's face. Instead, she laid it down while she tied her black tennis shoe.

"You don't have a sign," she said.

Kenika smiled. "Pisces is my sign."

The woman glared over her glasses. "You're not taking this serious. Damn millennials."

"Do you hear yourself? More than half of us here are millennials and Gen-Zers." Kenika wiped her damp face. "This is heavy stuff, a break here and there, a smile, a grin doesn't hurt."

She squinted against the sunlight to spy a tattoo on the older woman's neck. It bore three blackened teardrops arranged in a triangle. When the older woman stood, she cast a disgusted glance at Kenika, snatched up her sign and shouted, "*No justice! No peace!*"

"What's her problem?" Renee emerged from one of the portable bathrooms. Her dreadlocked hair swung in its ponytail. Its blonde tips brushed her shoulders. She stared after the woman until the crowd swallowed her.

"I dunno." Kenika clasped Renee's hand, and the two melded in with the others.

The day clotted over with thick clouds and humidity. Coupled with the packed streets, downtown became a hotbed of ignited tempers and short fuses.

"*Move, punk!*"

"*No justice! No Peace!*" came a shouted retort.

It took Kenika a minute to recognize the hollering came from the older woman.

The woman with the strange tattoo.

"Her again." Kenika tugged Renee's hand and drew her away from the argument erupting between the woman and a police officer. The hairs on the back of her neck stood in alarm. She didn't want to be anywhere near them if the powder keg exploded.

The throng parted to make room, to give air, perhaps to extinguish the rising altercation, but oxygen fueled fires, it didn't put them out.

And this was no different.

"Just get back!" The officer's riot gear skewed his face, but Kenika could tell by the voice and the temperament, he was male. He raised his baton and pointed to the crowd.

"Hey! She's not doing anything wrong!" a demonstrator shouted from the sea of faces.

Another added, "It's still a free country!"

"Leave her alone!"

The chorus swelled to a verbal tsunami. Other officers came to aid the protesters, and the gathering of dark-uniformed cops stood against those with dark-colored skin. Some had those strange tattoos on their necks. Heightened tensions guaranteed a scuffle would break out.

"This is about to pop off!" Renee yelled from beside Kenika, her grip tightening.

"I know." Kenika scanned the area for an escape route, or some place to wait out the approaching storm.

The other side of the street held restaurants, shops, and side streets some protestors had utilized to break away. Trickles of signs, people, and masks decorated the pavement.

"Come on." Kenika shouldered through the people. She popped out on the side street, along with Renee and a few others. The street sloped upward on an incline, and as Kenika made her way up, fleeing to higher ground, she turned to witness the unfolding incident below.

The protestors' tenor remained unsettled. The increasing swell of police officers, black beetles scurrying to the side street, blocked out the sidewalk and pushed—with their presence—the demonstrators to remain on the street. Plastic shields acted as temporary barriers, boxing the people into a makeshift pen, like animals on a farm, or sheep awaiting slaughter.

"What's with those strange tattoos? A whole lotta peeps had them." Renee rubbed the back of her neck, as if forcing the raised hair to lie down.

Kenika shook her head. "I dunno. I don't like the feeling of this."

"Me either." Renee looked up at the sky. "It's getting dark."

"It's only four o'clock." Kenika checked her fitness watch and then noted how gloomy everything looked. "It looks like we 'bout to get a little squall."

Thunder rumbled, and shortly thereafter a lightning flashed.

Summer storms in the south came with the humidity and the mosquitos. This, somehow, felt different.

"We gotta find shelter." Kenika elbowed Renee. "Over there."

One of the stores, a tiny used bookstore, sat with its door ajar and its sign switched to OPEN. The rest of the businesses had closed and boarded the windows in anticipation of the riot a certain news station promised would befall them. Kenika had always found solace among books, libraries, and such places, so she and Renee retreated.

The rumbling of raised voices, bullhorns, and shouting followed them.

THE STORM SPOOLED, WINDING THE PARTIES INTO an ever-tightening circle, until thick cords snapped like lightning, cracking across the heavens, splitting the sky.

The march was no different. Puddles of ruined lives, rippling into nowhere. Lives gobbled up by fear and loathing, leaving behind picked-over bones ravaged by vultures for five-second soundbites and two-second hot takes.

"WHAT'S GOING ON OUT THERE?" AN ELDERLY shopkeeper appeared from one of the stacks. She wore a long muumuu with geometric designs and a matching headwrap. Around her neck, she wore round, quarter-size beads and chains, a mixture of painted wooden balls and gold and silver links. She smelled like weathered wood and strong jasmine incense. "I hear there's gonna be a riot."

"Riot is the voice of the unheard," Renee said, as she tucked her hands into her shorts' pockets.

"Oh, yes," the woman agreed. "Come in."

Kenika followed Renee farther into the store. Once they did, the shopkeeper closed it, locked it, and flipped the sign to CLOSED.

Kenika stiffened.

The shopkeeper caught her body language. "Relax. It is merely a precaution to keep us safe from the storm."

"The storm?" Renee looked out the big display window. "They said it wouldn't rain today. That's why they went ahead with the march. Today's supposed to be perfect."

"All the same, I do not want the books to get wet in a sudden downpour." The shopkeeper gestured toward the book aisles and gave them an empty-mouth smile. A light switched on inside a back room.

It didn't put Kenika at ease. Instead, she took Renee's hand and backed away.

"Is it okay if we look around?" Kenika wanted to be free from the woman's dark, intense eyes. It was like she could feel the actual eyeballs on her skin. Her flesh crawled in response. Kenika took another involuntary step backward.

"Of course. Name's Althea. You'll find everything you need here."

Kenika walked down the first aisle of books, labeled *New Releases*. She hadn't been in a bookstore in ages, and the thrill of discovery vibrated through her. Now, out from underneath the strange Althea's gaze, she and Renee scanned the spines, their fingers tracing over the creative works put to paper. Each with the ability to teleport them to another place, another time, another world, even deeper into *this* one.

From outside, something exploded. The sound burst through the store's quiet interior with a spray of screams, gunfire, and sirens.

"Storm's here," Aletha declared from somewhere in the stacks.

"Yeah, it is." Kenika met Renee's raised eyebrows and widened eyes.

On the heels of the explosion, sirens and screams rent the shocked silence that followed. Kenika took out her cellphone and searched for a live news report and social media updates.

"They're teargassing the crowd. There's children and babies down there!" Kenika looked up at Renee's horrified face. "What the hell are they doing?"

"What they've always done. Trying to kill us." Renee hugged herself.

Althea rounded the corner and came up to them midaisle. "This storm will not be the last, nor will it continue for long. Short summer showers break off easily."

Althea handed a box of tissue to Renee.

It was then Kenika saw the three dark tears arranged in a triangle on her wrist.

Kenika accepted the box from Renee. "You're one of those…"

"People," Althea finished for her.

Kenika nodded, too numb to say anything more.

Renee looked at Kenika, who gestured toward her neck, and pointed at Althea.

Following Kenika's miming, Renee found her voice first. "We saw someone else with that tattoo. Is it some sort of gang or religious thing?"

"Yes and no," Althea said with a shrug.

"That's not an answer," Renee said.

Gunshots snared their attention. Kenika crouched to the floor, snatching Renee down with her. Althea remained standing, tall as a tree and with a stillness Kenika only saw in church women, holy women, who knew God stood by their side, unflinching and undeterred.

"Pellets from the storm." Althea walked to the front of the store.

"She's not serious," Kenika whispered to Renee. She pushed herself up on her knees. Althea stood at the door; palms pressed against the glass. A humming sound reverberated from her—or was it through her—and Kenika shuddered at the feel of it. The hum's energy rippled outward and washed over them. Renee gagged and slapped her hand over her mouth.

Kenika pulled her into an embrace and held her. Together, the nausea subsided, but Kenika didn't quite understand why the woman's humming bothered them in the first place. She held Renee close and rocked a little back and forth.

"We're safe. We're okay." Kenika didn't know how much of that she believed, but Renee needed to hear it.

Hell, *she* did too.

Outside, the gunfire stopped. The shouting and yelling didn't. Even though the action occurred down on the main road, the anguish echoed to them in the bookstore. Renee pressed herself closer into Kenika as if she meant to merge with her. She had both hands over her ears and fat tears rolled down her face.

"People are probably dying out there," Renee mumbled against Kenika's shoulder.

"We're safe. We're okay. We don't know if anyone has died, only gunshots. They could've been warning shots or rubber bullets."

Inside, Kenika groaned. Rubber bullets maimed and disfigured anyone they hit. All the police's non-lethal projectiles and weaponry became lethal in their hands.

Althea appeared above them, her shadow casting them in gloom. "Is your friend okay?"

Kenika swallowed to ease the lump of fear in her throat. "Yeah. Yeah. She's fine."

Those eyes moved from Kenika to Renee and back again. The shopkeeper didn't believe her. Kenika licked her lips and tried again. "She used to be a soldier, and stuff like this upsets her, okay? She's fine. Just, uh, give us a minute. Okay?"

"Of course." Althea drifted off to the front once more.

Kenika spied a chair and guided Renee to it. She sat her

in the chair and bent down beside her. "I'm going to go take a look around, but you're safe here—in this store. Do not leave. Call me on my cellphone and I'll be right back."

Renee snatched a fistful of Kenika's t-shirt. "Don't go out there."

Kenika wrapped her hand around Renee's trembling fist. "It's okay. I'm only going to the edge of the street, not all the way down. I wanna see if we can leave safely to go home. Then I'll nip right back here."

"She's right. You should stay inside while the storm is raging," Althea declared, spooking Kenika to a standing position.

"We need to get home. The march is over, she's sick, and we need to go." Kenika didn't dare meet the woman's penetrating gaze. It made her feel guilty all over.

"You're safe here."

I wish I could believe that.

"I know it seems strange here, but you trust me. You and your friend are quite safe here."

"We need to know what's going on." Kenika steadied herself by placing one hand on a neighboring shelf.

"What should be top of mind, for you and Renee, is your continued safety. Down there, police and protestors are engaged in one hell of a squall. Can't you hear the rumbling? The pellets of rain smacking against the ground?"

"That's a riot." Kenika shook her head.

"What is a storm but two opposing, powerful forces clashing for dominance? In this case, hatred and equality, justice and authority, equity and tyranny." Althea gestured toward the window. "If you must see with your own eyes, do, but know by crossing the store's threshold, you may not be able to return until the storm is at its end."

From behind Althea, Renee stood and mouthed the word, *no*.

"You promise she'll be safe here." Kenika forced herself to look Althea in the eye.

"Of course."

Kenika hesitated, but then pushed through the door and out into the unfurling gale.

***

THE SHARP ODOR OF TEARGAS FORCED KENIKA to weep as she made her way down the sidewalk and closer to the unfolding terror. Through watering eyes, she spied scattered bodies, splattered blood, and battered signs left in the storm's wake. Light rain made everything wet. She put her nose in the crook of her arm and tried not to breathe too deeply. Groaning, wailing, and deep moaning melded into an agonizing song. As the wind blew the noxious gas away from the street, it revealed those anguishing vocalizations to be from—the police.

Dozens of officers lay like crushed insects across the road and sidewalks. EMTs swarmed around them, wrapping injuries, and rolling out gauze, patching up those with minor injuries and hoisting the critical into ambulances. Firetrucks parked, marking off the scene. It looked like a war zone or the aftermath of Mother Nature's rage.

"What happened?" Kenika grabbed a passing pedestrian by the arm.

The woman turned to her, eyes wide, lips trembling, her

headband askew. "I-I dunno. They gassed us and then all I heard was screams. Oh, GOD, the screaming." She pressed her hands to her ears and cringed. "I ran. I ran as fast as I could."

"So, you dunno what happened to these people? The demonstrators?" Kenika gently shook the woman to halt the rising hysteria. "What did you see?"

The woman opened her eyes and shook her head. "I didn't see anything."

She snatched herself free and hurried down the sidewalk.

Kenika jumped as a hand fell onto her shoulder. She shook it off and rounded on the individual with her fist raised.

"Walk with me." The older woman she'd met earlier with the three teardrops neck tattoo started moving farther into the chaos.

Stunned, Kenika followed. The woman looked as if she'd been in a bloodbath. An abrasion on her forehead sealed itself before Kenika's eyes. Scarlet splatter covered her once-purple t-shirt and some had gotten in her hair. *Was that brain matter dangling from her ear?*

"I dunno what happened, but you should see one of the EMTs or go to the hospital."

The older woman said, "It isn't mine. None of it is mine."

Kenika swallowed and nodded at the officers. "So-o it's theirs."

"Yeah."

"Then why are we walking around them?" Kenika whispered. "You're covered in it. We're going to get arrested for assault, possibly murder."

The older woman grinned, a big, wide cold one. "Calm. Down."

Kenika's hand shot up. "Okay. Easy."

"Follow me."

"Yes, ma'am."

"Call me Suneeta."

They weaved through the chaotic scene. Kenika stepped over downed officers, through the acidic lingering odor of teargas, and around faint coppery pools of drying blood. The carnage made her sick to her stomach, but she didn't dare stop or race back to the bookstore.

No one spoke to them. No one stopped them. No one *saw* them.

Once they reached the small overpass bridge, Suneeta stopped.

Clustered there, groups of what looked like other demonstrators spoke in low tones, but all of them sported dried blood and other fluids and flesh from the storm. It was if they all got caught in a sudden summer downpour. They'd retreated from the squall to this location.

"I'm a member of the Drops." The older woman jutted her finger over her shoulder to a group of people standing together in a loose circle. "We go to all the marches and make sure the protestors are protected."

Kenika noticed the matching purple shirts from Suneeta to the others. They all bore the same neck tattoos, too. Were they some violent biker gang, like Hell's Angels, escorting abuse victims safely to their destination?

"I heard you asking questions..." Suneeta said.

"I—I don't need to know. I just wanna get myself and

my girl home." Kenika went with honesty, and she had a feeling Suneeta would appreciate it.

"She's with Althea, safe and sound."

"How did you know…" The question escaped before Kenika could stop it.

Suneeta licked her lips. "We're all connected." She tapped the tattoo. "Now, we gonna be gone here in a few, so let me go ahead and spell it out for you. I know you young folk ain't got a lot of critical thinking."

Kenika opened her mouth and then closed it at once. Her role here didn't include talking, but listening. So, she did.

"It's simple. We protect ours." Suneeta waved her hand toward the others. "Today, the cops wanted to reach out with batons and tasers to silence us. Can you believe it? So, we changed their tune."

"You beat them? Attack the cops?" Kenika thought back to the sheer violence delivered on the police.

"No. We *never* start it, only finish it." Suneeta grinned. Cracked blood flecked off her cheeks.

"This only makes us as bad as them. This doesn't separate us from them," Kenika said. She bit her lip and readied herself to run.

"You saw, but you didn't see." Suneeta shook her head in disappointment.

What was I supposed to see beyond the violence, the carnage, the chaos?

"I swear our public schools have failed us," Suneeta said. "If we hadn't been here, people would've died…"

"Those police officers *are* people—"

"Oh no," Suneeta said, her voice lowering an octave.

"Those were ghouls. Sucking out hope, life, and joy from folks."

Kenika *did* step back. "They're what?"

"Ghouls, and we are eternal night made flesh." Suneeta walked in a circle and whirled as if on a catwalk. "We are eternal, and we protect those who cannot protect themselves."

Kenika didn't know whether to laugh or cry. Something akin to a whimper escaped her lips, a mashup of both. Suneeta and the others had to be nuttier than a fruitcake. She had to get back to Renee.

"Great. Thanks, I gotta go." Kenika shot a fast fake smile and started back the way they'd come.

She'd kicked the bookstore door in, grab Renee, and hurry the fuck outta there.

"Where you goin'?" Suneeta flashed in front of her.

Startled, Kenika stumbled backward, catching herself before she fell.

"Don't you wanna know more?" Suneeta flashed white teeth, with long incisors.

Did your dentist do that to you? Kenika had read online how some people believed themselves to be vampires, so they did all sorts of things to their teeth to make it seem as if they had real fangs. They drank blood and dressed the part of an Anne Rice novel. Some even killed, but riot-clad cops?

"I—I have to get back." Kenika forced strength and calm she didn't feel into her words. Her insides quaked, and she wanted to vomit. Adrenaline made everything sharp and acidic.

"Stay with us a little longer." Suneeta clasped her on the

shoulder and the viselike grip kept her planted there. "What's your hurry again?"

"My girl..."

"Is tucked into a comfortable bookstore. You know what, Kenika. Why don't you join us?"

"Join your..." *Gang* sounded offensive. *Cult*, even worse.

"Club." Suneeta finished for her. "Most people run from us, from the naked violence, but you returned to it. I walked you through bloodied bodies, and you didn't even flinch or puke."

Kenika steadied herself. Suneeta couldn't be serious. Join? No.

"Thank you for the offer, but I—I need to think about it." Kenika tried to free herself from Suneeta.

"You do that." Suneeta peered at her. "We'll be here. We've always been here. Shepherding Harriet, counseling Martin, protecting Barack, and, well, now, ensuring Kamala's survival. Take your time."

Chills skated down Kenika's back.

On the one hand, it sounded like some internet Illuminati nonsense, but on the other hand, the flash of fang and the debris left on the downtown street were very real.

"Sure."

Suneeta released her, and it was as if a boulder had been lifted from her shoulder.

Kenika took a deep breath and bolted from the underpass. Her feet thudded against the cracked pavement, heart thundering like wild horses in her chest, thighs burning with effort to reach Renee.

Renee.

Kenika reached the bookstore's closed door. Before she touched the door handle, an energy beam jolted through her forearm and up to her shoulder. The smell of burnt flesh hit her nose. Her fingertips were black.

"What the hell is this?" Kenika peered inside the window. "Renee! Renee! I'm here!"

The finger of worry inched up her spine. She rubbed her head to dispel the crawling skin and the sense of unease. Anxiety and anguish flooded her system, and she felt sick as Althea's words came rushing back. They punched through the brain fog, hitting Kenika in her emotional center.

"No, no. Renee! Althea! Let me in!" Kenika tried to bang on the window, but once more, the energy sent her windmilling back, across the sidewalk and into the street.

Overhead, dusk descended, and the already dark afternoon began to meld into night. The blue and red flashes of light rotated across the area, a macabre disco ball with the dead dancing on their corpses. She cried out. Pain pulsated through every fiber of her body.

"Kenika." Althea emerged from the shadows, eyes glowing like hot coals, afro reaching to the ceiling. She fingered her necklace.

A stillness borne of the cemetery draped like a cold breeze around them. "I'm back. Send Renee out. All's clear."

"You're panicked and anxious. She's safe. I told you." Althea smiled.

It was meant to be reassuring.

It wasn't.

Kenika approached the door as close as she dared. "I

appreciate it. Now, send her out. Please." She fought to keep her voice from trembling. The itch to push the door open caused her hands to quiver. She rolled them into fists to steady them.

Althea's grin dropped. "I did warn you about leaving..."

"What did you do to her?" Kenika shook her fist at the shopkeeper. *I knew she'd do something to Renee. I shouldn't have left her. Damn, I should've listened to my gut.*

"We're shepherds, not wolves."

Althea waved her right hand. The interior lights flickered on, revealing Renee, seated in the blue reading chair Kenika had left her in.

"Renee! It's me!" Kenika waved her hands and jumped up and down to snare her partner's attention. Kenika looked at Althea. "What did you do to her?"

"She sees and hears you." Althea glanced over her shoulder to the seated woman.

"Then why doesn't she answer me?"

"She doesn't want to come out. She's comfortable and safe here." Althea turned her back to Kenika. "Good evening."

"No!" Kenika shot forward. An electric jolt knocked her into the street. "Renee!"

The bookstore lights winked out, and Althea bled into the dark without another word.

What have I done?

The flood of acid raced up her throat, and she sunk to her knees, fighting back tears and the urge to vomit. Her stomach knotted in agony at the flood of possible thoughts racing through her. *Is she dead? Did they hurt her? Oh, God! I left her alone. I thought she was safe!*

Kenika screamed, sinking to her knees.

Renee!

Kenika rubbed her head and sat down on the curb outside the bookstore. Streetlights popped on and light traffic drove up and down the street. Perhaps pride or her family's legendary stubbornness kept her rooted there. Leaving didn't occur to her as an option, not without Renee.

"Ma'am." A voice roused her from her musings.

"Yeah?" Kenika looked to find it belonged to a uniformed officer standing above her.

"You'll need to move along." He gestured with one hand. His other rested on his gun belt.

"Why? I'm just sitting here." Kenika saw the fear in his wide eyes as he took in her march t-shirt. She spoke in a calm tone. "I'm waiting for my friend."

He didn't hear any of it. "Head on home, ma'am."

"I have a right to sit here. I'm not disturbing anyone. All of these stores are closed."

"You're loitering."

"There's not a no-loitering sign here. This is a shopping area."

"Ma'am." The officer's hand eased to his handgun.

Kenika tensed. Her mouth went dry. She raised her hands in the don't shoot position.

"I'm standing up," she announced.

She felt like she wanted to puke, but fleeing would definitely get her a bullet in the back.

"I'm not gonna tell you again. Go. Home." The officer then spoke in lowered tones into his radio.

"Everything okay, Kenika?" Suneeta's powerful voice bowled through the gathering dark crafted by the streetlights.

Relief washed over Kenika.

Suneeta stopped behind the cop. He turned so he could see them both with his back to the store's door. Althea came to the front, and the lights came on, pouring illumination on the scene.

"Hello, officer," Althea said.

It occurred to Kenika that she, Suneeta, and Althea formed a triangle, and the tattoo made sense. All three Black women, who'd shed more tears than anyone in history.

"Ma'am." The police officer nodded at Althea. "Um, you ladies be careful out here."

"Oh, we will be," Suneeta said.

He must have seen something in her face because he hurried down the sidewalk.

"Thank you." Kenika sagged as adrenaline slowed.

Suneeta flashed fangs. "That's what we do."

Kenika looked at Althea to Suneeta. "Did y'all set this up to get me to join?"

Suneeta shook her head. "Girl, there's so much rampant malice and hatred, we don't need to create scenarios."

Kenika said to Althea. "Where's Renee?"

Althea opened the door. "Right here."

Renee crept around Althea and out to the sidewalk.

"I'm sorry. I needed more time to get myself together." She hurried to Kenika and embraced her.

She smelled like lavender and leaves, fire, and cinnamon. Most important of all, she felt good in Kenika's arms.

Everyone should feel this safe, this blessed, this loved.

Over Renee's shoulder, Kenika opened her eyes and met Suneeta's gaze. She broke the embrace and cleared her throat.

"Okay. I'm in," Kenika said to Suneeta.

Suneeta glanced at Althea and then back to Kenika. "Good. Every herd needs good shepherds to get them through the storms."

LIPSTICK SMILE

"Although the sun shines, there are always shadows." Kimra sidestepped yet another face-glued-to-their-cellphone person doing their zombie walk down the corridor inside Southgate Mall in Charlotte.

The late Saturday afternoon witnessed a surge in younger folks and a decline in authentic adults. The big mall anchor store announced its new sale in large, screaming yellow and red signage that shot out of the mall's floor in metallic stands and plastered posters across most of the surfaces not already covered.

"Do you ever get tired of being gloomy? You're so damn depressing." Vega frowned, making her elegantly drawn, colored, and gelled brows wrinkle. Well, not the eyebrows so much as the skin around them. Her best friend since elementary school, Vega sailed through the crowd like a golden swan, graceful and swift.

"Nope. I'm happy when I'm sad," Kimra replied, fingering her afro puffs. She smirked at Vega.

"Damn, that's weird." Vega sucked her teeth and tossed her waist-long rainbow braids over her shoulders. Everything about her glowed, from her gold bangles on her wrists, to her gold earring hoops that brushed her shoulders, and on to her layered gold necklaces around her neck.

"That's okay. I'm goin' get you whipped into shape." Vega pursed her lips with the promise. "You live in Kannopolis, home to all the beautiful people."

"I like my shape just the way it is." Kimra pinched her love-handles and shook them at Vega.

She smirked, shaking her head. "But you got such a pretty face."

Kimra'd been hearing that her whole life. It played like a well-worn laugh track. She'd been a chubby baby, a thick teenager, and now a "curvy" woman. "Real women have curves," the television bellowed, but then in a whisper, "... but not too much."

"I have an amazing personality." Kimra shoved her hands into her joggers' pockets. When her hands started to ache, she realized they'd been clenched into tight fists.

"Shush. I got you." Vega swept her hands toward the store ahead of them.

They arrived at the mouth of the large, carnivorous department store. Here, the ugly and unsophisticated entered, their identities devoured by the make-up counters, personal shoppers, and salons.

What remained was cookie cutter culture. Kimra paused at the mouth of the department store. A sliver of worry wiggled down her spine. Vega kept walking a few feet before she realized that Kimra wasn't with her.

"Kimmie? Girl, come on!"

Her voice sounded muffled, but Kimra could make it out. The lights flickered behind Vega. The store seemed to be cackling at her hesitation, daring her to enter.

"I dunno, Vega. I love my face like it is." Kimra hated the

sharp whine wrapped around her words. It bored holes in her resolve. The pleading made her sick to her stomach.

"Nuh huh. You'd be happy if you did." Vega snorted. "I know you, Kimmie. You just thirstin' for knowledge."

"I don't want strange knowing, like what's in there." Kimra nodded in the department store's direction. "The secrets of beauty, making yourself skinny and creating man-made glamour."

"Everyone wants glamour. I'm not judging you, but we did talk about this already. You said you'd try." Vega's tone was light, but her nostrils flared, signaling her annoyance.

"Yeah," Kimra whispered. She'd confronted Vega with the facts, but that hardly mattered. Vega was always the life of the party. This visit to the mall was no different.

"Oh, I know. Let's split the difference. A new lipstick would do wonders to brighten you up." Vega sparkled despite the shadows lingering and looming in and out of the department store's gaping entrance.

Kimra wondered if the shadows would return to human forms once they exited the mall. Shopping bags seemed too heavy for ghostly arms and rotting hands.

"I've never liked lipstick." Kimra quirked an eyebrow at Vega. They'd backed off the full facial makeover. So she *was* making headway.

"Why not? You already wear lip gloss. Think of lipstick as a fancy lip gloss," Vega reassured her. A warm glow, an aura, softly pulsated around Vega. "It's fun. Come on, scaredy cat."

Another chill raced up her spine, reversing course. Kimra straightened, threw back her shoulders, and faced the store. She could do this. Lipstick was just glorified lip balm. That she could do, a tiny sacrifice to the gods of beauty.

"Let's get some color in your face." Vega guided her toward the entrance.

I'm Black. I already have color, courtesy of Mother Melanin, Kimra thought, but didn't say. She hurried along, propelled by Vega's pace and guiding hand. They entered into the stunning fluorescent illumination. Kimra winced, but peered through slits as Vega led her to the equally bright beauty counter.

"Hello. Welcome to Marv's," said the slender, hollow-cheeked woman draped in a blood red dress with platform heels. Her name tag said Linda. "How can I help?"

Vega met the store clerk's wolfish grin. "Hey, Linda. We're looking at lipsticks."

Linda rubbed her pale, slender hands together. The grin remained. Kimra wondered if it was detachable, like the store nametag. She rebuked herself. *You can't always trust first impressions.*

"We have a sale on facials. You like one?" Linda asked.

Too many teeth. Kimra shuffled behind Vega and swiftly turned her face away. She couldn't look at the beauty clerk. For starters, Linda's sheet of perfect brunette hair captured the light, trapping it like a spider with a web. Secondly, Linda's flawlessly crafted face was beautiful and terrifying. Too many teeth crowded into a too-small mouth. Too perfect. She looked capable of something cruel.

"No! Thank you!" Kimra said, before Vega answered for her.

Linda's mouth widened, if that was possible. Kimra

shuddered, cursing herself for taking a peek. The heavy cloak of perfume made her stomach hurt even more. Something coppery and acidic flavored the air, looming beneath the manufactured aromas.

Kimra closed her eyes and opened them after summoning the remnants of her courage and the protection of her ancestors. *Ready.*

"Just. Lipstick," Kimra said, on the edge of bolting.

Vega laughed. "She's new to this."

"I see. Fresh meat," Linda purred, rolling the R in fresh like her tongue wanted to make love to it. The way she said it made Kimra's skin break out in gooseflesh.

The golden-capped lipsticks were lined in a row, round for sampling, corralled for plucking. Linda's long fingers glided across the luminous rainbow colors. The retail ones hid under the counter in individual boxes, mass produced for consumption.

Linda eyed Kimra's mouth. "Such beautiful lips, full and plump. No enhancements."

Kimra blanched, if her dark skin could do such a thing. The hairs on the back of her neck stood at rigid attention. Those words scared the daylights out of her. She turned, but Vega caught her by the elbow and pulled her forward. Linda's mouth watered. The clerk patted the sides of her mouth with a napkin, and her grin returned.

"Try these." Linda splayed the lipsticks across the glass counter. "Your skin is so luscious. Do you know? Clear. Vibrant." She licked her lips a moment before the teeth came back into view.

Vega elbowed her. "See? Told you."

Kimra met Vega's smile and tried to relax. "Okay. Let's do the purple one first."

Vega grunted and shot Kimra an encouraging nod.

Kimra picked up the tiny tube and leaned in to the large circular mirror. With a quick push of her thumb, she uncapped the disposable sampler.

"Oh, yes! The Deadly Nightshade," Linda cooed, pleasure making her eyebrows rise higher above her artfully decorated and glistening dark eyes.

Kimra froze, the cap in one hand, the sampler in the other. "Isn't that poisonous?"

Vega interjected. "Only in large dosages. I'm kidding! They're just names. There ain't no real nightshade in there."

But Kimra watched Linda, who remained silent, wearing the too-many-teeth grin, her gaze trained on Kimra's every move.

"Lovely shade. Put. On," Linda encouraged after several tense moments.

Was it her, or was Linda struggling with simple language?

"I'm going to try this one," Kimra said and recapped the purple one. Maybe it was her imagination, but Linda's smile had sharp edges that drooped in disappointment when she declined the purple lipstick.

Kimra opened the red matte color. With her heart pounding, she ran the sampler across her lips, turning them from their natural, healthy roseate to a deep crimson.

"Venom looks brilliant on you," Linda exclaimed; a small vein snaking down her forehead stood out in excitement.

"Oooh, Venom," Vega chided. She spun her around to face her. "Beautiful."

"Show me," Linda hissed.

Did this woman know any other words?

Linda's outstretched hand twitched in anticipation but paused, just shy of touching Kimra. Kimra didn't think she wanted Linda touching her. In fact, she was certain, but she turned to face Linda, anyway. The rail-thin clerk greedily clasped her hands together once Kimra came into her full focus.

Kimra spied her own reflection, from the corner of her eye, in the mirror. It was her. Then again, at the same time, it wasn't. What she saw made her blood run cold. Her eyes, her chin, her nose all looked the same, original Kimra. But her lips had peeled back, revealing a mouth crammed with teeth overlapping each other. The front top teeth elongated and dripped with saliva against the backdrop of crimson. Bleak. Gruesome.

Kimra reached up to touch her lip. Panic flooded her chest. She struggled to breathe. "What the hell?"

"Don't!" Linda slapped her hand, no longer the bubbly makeup counter clerk.

"Ow!" Kimra scowled and rubbed the back of her hand.

"Leave your beauty. Don't remove it." Linda's eyes widened as she further declared, "This color has flair."

Vega cocked her head to the side. "Kimmie, dial it back!"

"That is what I said!" Linda laughed, hollow and empty like her eyes, like a casket after a thousand years of buried decay.

Kimra caught chills again, backed away from the

counter, and looked around for Vega. "V, do you see this right here?"

But suddenly Vega wasn't there.

Her best friend had melted into the throng of shoppers, leaving her alone. As she whirled slowly around, scanning the seas of faces swimming by, Kimra's stomach balled into nausea. Had she really ever been here? *Vega?* Had she actually come here alone? But why would she do that?

Kimra didn't know any more.

"Ah, do not be afraid. You look gorgeous!" Linda gestured her to come back to the counter. She blinked; unrealistic eyelashes brushed her upper cheeks. "There's no solace in beauty, only pain."

The words called up such terror, it enveloped Kimra in its tight embrace. Every fiber roared with alarm, but Kimra drifted forward as if Linda held her mouth by a tether. Was she facing something sinister? Surely not at a department store's makeup counter. Kimra spied her face again and noted the hideous smile etched into it. The fear gripped her again.

"No! Get this off me! I'm not interested in pain!" Kimra rushed the last few steps to the counter, snatched up the tissues from the box, and wiped her lips until they were raw.

"Try another? Facial?" Linda asked, gesturing to the ever-expanding circle of cosmetics appearing on the counter.

Kimra shook her head, too scared to vocalize an answer. She realized that Linda's struggle to speak came from the overabundance of teeth in her mouth. Scared, Kimra tried not to allow it to root her there. She started backing away. Her heart pounded against her chest like it worked at a disco.

"Wait! Sale! Special!" Linda's long, pale arms shot out

like vines, but with nails like claws, swatting the air in attempts to snare her.

Kimra thought again about the spider, spinning more web to stop the fidgeting prey from moving, escaping.

"No! No!" Kimra backpedaled faster. Too afraid to put her back to the store clerk, Kimra kept moving, bypassing shadows and face-planted-in-screen zombies. Her throat was too dry for her to say more, so her hands waved Linda off until she plowed into something solid.

"Watch it, there!" Vega's husky voice shouted in irritation. "You could lose a body around these parts."

"Where have you been?" Kimra screamed. Fury rolled forward, making her face hot. She grabbed Vega's shoulders and shook her gently.

"Um, clearly we're still fine-tuning our boundaries, Kimmie." Vega shrugged her off. "What happened to your lips? They're bleeding."

"That lipstick! It's horrid!" Kimra touched her sore lips and cringed. "Where were you?"

Vega shrugged. "Damn. I spent a lot of emotional equity on this trip to Linda."

Perhaps finding the anger burning in Kimra's face, Vega dropped her gaze and mocking tone.

"Okay, sorry! Something grabbed my attention. I got carried away looking at jewelry. Calm down. I left you in good hands." Vega spoke with all the care of one who just lost a sock.

"Linda?" Kimra shook her head.

Vega shrugged again. "Yeah. She's no-pressure sales and a free spirit."

"Demonic spirit is what you mean," Kimra said.

As they exited the department store, Kimra released a breath she didn't even know she was holding. Still, a touch of foreboding made her pause. Vega waved her on. They took the side door exit to the parking lot. Finally, the numbness faded from her lips.

Vega gave her a side-eye glance and shrugged, though her plans to get Kimra to wear makeup had hit a snag. "Still free."

"About that, Vega, we got a little more to discuss," Kimra said, a bit unsure if she should convey what she'd seen. They fell silent as they walked through the parking lot to Vega's car.

Kimra buckled her seatbelt and waited for Vega to start the car. Vega lowered the driver's side visor and flicked up the mirror. Outside, a soft rain fell. In the glistening surface of the water drenched pavement, the vehicles shimmered. In the twilight, the mirror's light flashed on. Vega pulled out her gold-capped lipstick from her purse.

"Vega, is that..."

"Yeah. This one is Blood Moon." Vega puckered and applied the lipstick with a practiced hand.

Kimra froze. *Now what?*

Her heart inched into her throat, even as her blood slowed in her veins. Next to her, Vega had this weird smile on her face. But Kimra only saw the profile view.

"V? Linda is a monster."

"Hmmm?" Vega slapped the visor back into place. *Whack!*

"A monster..." Kimra whispered, throat going dry.

"I'm not that kind of person. Yes, I became that person. This is not me," Vega said, before turning to Kimra and smiling, her rainbow braids spilling across her shoulders.

Filled with teeth.

"Ain't I pretty?" Vega leaned closer to Kimra, eyes glazed over, wide with wonder. "Ain't I?"

Kimra screamed and tried to melt into the passenger-side door. Her hands couldn't seem to get a grip on the latch.

With eyes as large as saucers and nostrils flared, Vega leaned over the gearshift, saliva dripping down the corners of her too-broad smile. "This. Is. Love-ly. Yeah?"

Kimra shut her eyes tight. "No beauty is worth this!"

A soft humming took up residence in her ears, and she tried to ball herself into a tight knot. Maybe, just maybe, if she prayed enough, she'd wake up in her bed.

Minutes elongated, stretching out like the long canines in Linda's mouth. Shuddering in the still-hot car, Kimra emitted a "Please, Lordt," against the thick air.

"Kimmie?" Vega's voice sounded normal, not laced with gravel as it had a few minutes earlier. "You okay?"

Kimra peeked through her hands and then lowered them to find Vega scowling at her. "Girl, it ain't that hot. Give the air a minute."

Kimra sat up straight in her seat and looked around. Everything seemed normal, even Vega. She shook her head to clear the lingering cobwebs and chill of the encounter.

Had she imagined it? Been dreaming?

"I'm okay," she said, and then with more confidence, "I'm okay!"

Vega smirked at her as she shifted the car into reverse and backed out of the parking lot.

That's when Kimra spied the sprinkle of saliva dotting

the area around the gearshift. Vega didn't appear to notice it, and she put the car in drive. They headed off into Charlotte's clogged and congested streets.

Kimra swallowed the hard lump of fear down her dry throat.

As Vega drove, she said, "You know, we should check out the cosmetic counter over at the mall in Rock Hill..."

"No! No, I'm good!" Kimra screamed.

Vega flinched. "Wow! Well, okay. You know, you have such a pretty face..."

SIRENS' SONG

"You ever wanna just walk into traffic?"

Katrina cut her dark eyes over to me. Beneath the fall of her curly bangs, she sucked her teeth. "No. Of course not."

"Of course," I agreed, already sorry I mentioned it.

I did find it hard to believe she didn't hear the cars' song rushing by. It was definitely a song, not the harsh blaring of horns and rude honks. No, it was lyrical and enchanting. An open invitation to peace and solace.

Katrina adjusted her collar against the cold winter wind. "Stop being weird. I'm hungry."

We walked down the sidewalk along 12th Avenue. She hit my shoulder with hers like a bumper car. I shuffle closer to her, and that's when I heard it.

"It goes like this:
Come play with us,
It'll be fun.
Come play with us,
You'll be done.
Come play with us,
It'll be fine!
Come play with us,
Then you'll die."

Katrina shoved her gloved hands into her coat pockets and glared at me. "Mimi. Mimi?!"

"What?" I came back to myself, standing on the curb between a graffitied newspaper machine and a fire hydrant.

"I've been calling your name for like five whole minutes." She shook her head. "You kinda zoned out."

I gave a half-hearted smile. "Sorry about that. Something, uh, caught my attention."

The flat tone alarmed Katrina despite my efforts to give positive verbal cues. She grabbed my arm, spun me around, and with the distance between her artful eyebrows wrinkling, said, "Come on. It's cold. You don't really hear cars talking to you. Right?"

The false smile pulled tight on my lips. "No, girl. 'Course not. That's crazy."

She searched my face, her gaze roaming all over me like a thousand ants. I kept the smile in place until she relaxed. The bunched-up skin on her forehead smoothed.

"Okay. Let's go get some food. A good bowl of pho will chase off the chills," Katrina said, pulling my arm as she marched ahead.

I didn't want to get anything into me, but I allowed myself to be towed to the Vietnamese bistro on the corner. The cold helped me keep my face blank even though the aroma of rich beef broth was delicious. We'd ventured out for pho, our favorite meal, despite the cold December temperatures. We came to the intersection of 12th Avenue and Vine Drive. Pho Ngon sat glowing with illuminated lights and heated dining area. I turned to follow Katrina into the open door when I stopped.

I looked back to the street and the whispering that brushed my ears grew louder.

"Come play with us,
It'll be fun.
Come play with us,
You'll be done.
Come play with us,
It'll be fine!
Come play with us,
Then you'll die."

"Mimi," Katrina called from what seemed like a long tunnel. "We're letting all the heat out."

Harsh shouts in Vietnamese and English jerked me back to the here and now. I shook my head to dislodge the song, still softly echoing in my ears—an earworm for eternity. I forced a grin and walked into the pho restaurant. We waved at the owners' young son, David, who manned the seating area. He had already placed menus at our favorite table.

We ordered, not even bothering to look at the choices. I stared across at Katrina, pink with cold. She removed her woolen hat and her gloves. Her coat she'd ditched on the coatrack as soon as we came in. I had done the same, though I didn't remember doing so.

"You know, I know it's horrible. This whole year has been awful, but we can eat good food and enjoy the warmth of friendship." Katrina sipped her hot tea. She glanced up at me, concern a shadow on her face. "It'll be all right."

I nodded. My smile felt loose and empty. "Sure thing. It just needs time."

"Right."

David came with our meals and soon limes and chili

paste melded yummy pho into warm comfort. We ate in silence, Katrina having said all she could and my earworm replaying the song as if stuck on repeat.

After we paid, Katrina reapplied her woolen hat, gloves, and coat in preparation for a return to the cold.

I did too, but I didn't dread the wintry fingers slipping into my coat.

As we exited, I heard it again, louder than the last time, as the traffic light changed from red to green.

"Come play with us,
It'll be fun.
Come play with us,
You'll be done.
Come play with us,
It'll be fine!
Come play with us,
Then you'll die."

My heart raced, and my feet moved on their own, away from the restaurant. A prick of cold, more frigid than the winter temperature, rippled from my head to my booted feet, making me shiver. I let the door go, and I heard it faintly click shut.

Ahead, the stream of cars bolted through the intersection, shouting their song and extending their smear of colors and solace out toward me.

And I extended my hand, my body, my all to them.

The blaring and chorus of horns, shouts, and screams celebrated my decision.

SUNSHINE

"Keep your face to the sunshine and you cannot see a shadow."
—Helen Keller

Warmth burrowed through her thick blanket of sleep. It didn't ask permission for entry, but instead pushed aside slumber's all-encompassing hold, wrenching Geraldine into reality's harsh and cold embrace with complete indifference. A straight-up betrayal of the sun's promise to keep her warm.

Rude.

Geraldine rubbed her eyes and winced against the room's brightness. For most, sunlight meant life. Plants created food from it and people survived on their output, oxygen and food.

But for an unlucky few, the sun meant death.

As if demons could ever truly die. Geraldine pushed the thought aside as she sat up and nudged her tabby, Katrina, to the floor. Kat responded with an angry meow.

"I don't wanna be awake either." Geraldine pushed her dreadlocks back from her face.

Nevertheless, she was awake. Golden sunlight poured

through the parted blinds and into her private space. She stretched out her hands and touched a ray, twisting it in her fingertips as she pulled from the magic within herself. As she did so, the room's walls dissolved into bright light before reforming as the corner of the institution's stone block walls. From the blinds, the sun's rays shimmered and cast strange patterns across the hardwood floor and Geraldine's yellow bedding. Illuminated dust danced in the air and mixed with the heady scent of magic.

...And sulfur.

Demons.

She rolled out of bed, stretched, and tied her locks into a bun at the base of her neck. With her hands on full hips, she called out.

"Speak. I know you're here."

The shadows bulged and burst. A sizzling grew louder as a form solidified into a hazy silhouette.

Geraldine shook her head. "You demons suck at mimicking."

The shadow flickered and tightened into more of a human outline, forming a face with eyeless sockets.

"Come on, all damn ready. It's too early for this." Geraldine folded her arms and waited.

"Come. On. *Geee*." The huddled form's face split into a gaping mouth. Its voice mocked her in a travesty of antiquated urban slang.

"That's how you show respect? Get out. I'm going back to bed."

Without waiting to see if the entity complied, she climbed back into bed and waited. Kat co-signed on this course of action and leapt back onto the bed. She started kneading the covers, purring in anticipation, and prepping for another nap.

"Must you be cruel?" The echoing wheeze of their words filled the room.

Their voice made Geraldine's skin crawl. A thousand souls crushed in agony and amplified as one. She hated that they'd come to visit her—again. Each time attempting to provoke her into doing the one thing that would grant them pleasure—her death.

They wouldn't kill her. No, that wouldn't be nearly as satisfying as watching her mental torment and then, in glee, witnessing her taking her own life. Demons envied her human lineage and wanted her to be among them. A certain ticket she'd end up in Hell with them.

"Cruelty and honesty are hard to distinguish from each other, especially for your kind." She fluffed her pillow and turned back to face them.

"Our kind is *your* kind." Their arms gestured to her and then dissolved into the huddled form again.

Geraldine quirked an eyebrow at the comment. Rumors from her family had hinted at their lineage and part of their power coming from an evil source. She didn't believe it. Her momma hailed from a land drenched in the sun's power. They harnessed the universe's magic, the power from a star. Now she did too. Despite the golden orb's reluctance, she would pool the sunlight into power. Her momma spoke of how the sun despised being under their yoke, so it burned their flesh when they tried to absorb too much. When her skin captured its energy, she used it to ignite the magic inside her.

Geraldine sighed. Demons. Didn't they have other

things to do? With her palms raised, she called upon the cells in her body to conjure the magic in preparation for their possible attack. As she focused, her skin began to tingle.

The demons' poorly contrived physical presence shimmered in her bedroom's early morning glow. The situation must be dire for them to contact her during the day, when the sun was up.

"What do you want?" Geraldine repeated.

They wouldn't leave unless she at least allowed them to tempt her. That's the rule of how she ended up in this place; summoning demons to strengthen her own inherited powers had caused her to kill her best friend. Geraldine confided to her defense lawyers that the demons had tricked her, and now, she resided here. Each day, the demons came to try again.

But she'd make sure that today, once again, they failed. Once she'd done that, she'd send them back to the cozy lake of fire they slipped out from. Maybe then she'd get some sleep.

"We have a surprise for you," the demons declared.

"What?" Geraldine asked, but as soon as she did, three hard knocks burrowed through the door seconds before two large men dressed in white button-down shirts and matching pants rushed into the room.

"Why even bother knocking?" she said. *Not this again.* She turned to the demons. "You guys lack originality."

"Who you talkin' to?" Matthew, one of the orderlies, slammed his fist against the wall. "Or it's back to the padded room."

"Geraldine! My name's Geraldine!"

She balled up her fists, the hairs on her neck standing in

rapt attention. Beside her, Kat vanished into the sunlight's glow. The small rectangular room, narrow, and similar to other rooms in the institution, held everything she loved. Those things now dissolved into the sunlight.

With each step Matthew took, the blinds, the comfortable bedding—it all vanished, leaving only a wrought-iron bedframe, a thin mattress with scratchy sheets, and a threadbare rug.

Geraldine fought to slow her breathing and retain control as she slid out from her bed, watching the orderlies, Matthew in particular.

"What did I do this time?" The demons had sent them, she knew.

When she looked over to the mass of darkness masquerading as a person, she found them watching with rapt attention. Or so she imagined, since their concealed form had no facial features.

"It don't matter what you done or didn't do. You gonna do what I say." Matthew marched farther into her personal space.

"No." The word came out in a calm, enunciated syllable.

"No?" He folded his arms and smirked. "You what they call mentally ill, *Gerry*. Fucking crazy. You do what I tell you."

Gleams like sunshine in a brave man's eye.

Euripides's words echoed in Geraldine's mind as she watched the two men prepare to attack. Although dressed in white, their souls were stained with streaks of filth. They had been tasked with maintaining order in the institution. *As if.* They could barely handle breathing and walking at the same time.

She readied herself for the familiar game. Despite the seriousness of the situation, it *was* a game: a match between herself and the darkness, the demons.

"Aye, look, man, she got that wild stare again. Let's go." Rod, the other orderly, tugged on Matthew's shirt before he backed out of the room.

Geraldine could smell his acidic sweat—an indicator of his terror. He made a feeble attempt to take Matthew with him, but the larger orderly shook him off.

"Coward. We got a job to do," Matthew said over his shoulder.

Geraldine felt the oily demonic presence creep further into her room. Demons had life-eating powers. Drawn entirely by instinct, the spirits' vast and potent nature fed on human misery. None were more miserable than those in an insane asylum. The more emotional, the more horrific. The roar of the collective outrage of the deranged, the depraved, and the depressed echoed through her opened door. She understood why the demons came to torment her.

"Besides, she's a piece-of-shit head case." Matthew leered, his own fists drawn tight.

"It ain't right." Rod's voice quivered like a kite caught in a hell storm.

Rod and Matthew had become a sadistic show in constant replay. The bruising from their last round of "fun" hadn't yet changed into the sickening dark green of *healing* along her legs and arms.

She heard scuffling, their voices descending into grunts and grumblings before dissolving into a thousand souls crushed into one.

Demons.

Just as Rod regained his footing, Matthew slammed the door closed.

Geraldine's skin felt cold, so she turned to the warmth. When she reached toward the sun, her fingers brushed the rays and she felt instant joy.

She giggled.

"The hell you laughin' at, bitch?" Matthew jerked his shirt down where it had crept above his belly.

Geraldine ignored the buzzing noise, the sound of the demons' attempts to sync together, and Matthew. The sun's waves held much more promise than the dark shadow huddling inside her room, dressed in a white orderly uniform. The burning star offered power, hope, and above all, freedom.

Wham! The blow against her neck ignited a flare of pain and sent her crashing back onto the bed. The springs of the lumpy mattress hid just beneath the threadbare fabric. One of them scraped her cheek, drawing blood. With her cheek on fire and her back in agony, Geraldine had scarcely a moment to breathe before Matthew continued his assault by punching her in the back, slamming his fist into her kidney.

Geraldine didn't cry out. The days of screaming for a rescue, for a change, for someone in the institution to acknowledge the depravity that visited her room, had faded like the room's sun-bleached wallpaper. In those earlier dark years, when her screams had littered the corridors, the ceilings, and the walls, along with her spilled blood, through the fog of agony, a beacon had shone. Her power erupted, and she learned to use it.

Unafraid, Geraldine rolled off the bed, using the momentum Matthew had unleashed to her advantage. Now she had room to work. Breathing through the pain, she called upon her solar magic.

After all, she was made of stars.

The morning's sunlight streamed behind her, warming her back, her neck, and her hair, giving her strength despite her injuries as it did so. The sun poured its power into her, illuminating her, bringing her magic to her fingertips. She stood tall as she raised her palms to face him.

"Leave my space or face my fury."

His smudge of a face, blurred now as the demons' control over Matthew broke down, smiled.

"I ain't leavin'. This stinkin' place reeks of your *people's stink*."

"That's brimstone, and it hails from the home of YOUR people." With those words, she sent a magical blast of sunlight from her palms.

Matthew burst into a shower of dark gray balls before unifying again as one thick-headed orderly. The odor of burnt flesh rose in the air.

"Gonna wish you hadn't done that." Matthew launched himself at her.

Geraldine shuffled back, her shoulders bumping the windowsill. Matthew crashed onto the twin bed and pushed himself up, scurrying backward to his feet. Fists pounding the air, he came for her again. Determination shone in the sweaty gloss on his face.

She sidestepped his punch and whirled with a double-fisted magical slam of her own directly into his belly. It sent Matthew crashing to the concrete floor.

He yelped, and held his stomach as he tried to stand. The door banged open. Rod and two other orderlies came in with hesitant steps. Their faces registered their concern. Rod looked from Matthew to her and then back to him. Disbelief spoiled his features.

"Don't just stand there. Tie her up! She's got a weapon!" Matthew shouted, his face flushed from pain.

The two men moved to restrain her.

"If you're going to lie, be good at it. Otherwise, I get bored." Geraldine held her arms high in surrender, the stance of peace and protest.

"Wait!" Rod shouted to the others. He avoided her gaze. "She ain't got a weapon. Uh, Matt must be mixed up. You know, confused. Help 'im up and let's get outta here before the doctor come 'round. Almost time for group, anyway."

Matthew cursed. "Do what I tell you. Restrain her!"

Geraldine kept her hands high, but glanced over to the corner where the demons had been. Now, only golden light remained.

Rod shook his head. "What happened? Weapons ain't allowed, and she didn't have one when I came in."

Matthew scowled at him and the other orderlies.

Seconds felt like years before Matthew answered.

"Nothin'." He yanked his shirt down over his belly with an angry glare at Geraldine.

"Let's go." Rod waved them out of the room.

The men obeyed. When Matthew moved his hand, Geraldine saw the burnt edges of his clothing and the blistered flesh of his abdomen.

After the other three men filed out of her room in hushed silence, Rod cast a glance back at her before slamming the door shut. The lock scraped as it slid into place, signaling the end of the test.

Today, she'd won.

"People are capable of such horrific acts," Geraldine said to herself as she climbed onto her bed. Thick blankets and a bright yellow comforter materialized beneath her body. Fluffy and soft, it cushioned her now-aching limbs.

Kat meowed in obvious agreement from her spot on the hardwood floor. Polished, honey-brown wood gleamed in the light.

"Come on up." Geraldine patted the bed beside her.

Kat leapt onto the mounds of blankets. Once she found a spot, she lay beside Geraldine, a regal Egyptian cat, her green eyes peering across all she surveyed.

As the late-morning sunbeams brightened the room, her blinds reappeared, cloaking the thick, scarred metal bars along the institution windows. Ferns flourished once more from their potted locations along the top of her bookshelves.

With Kat's purring warmth nestled next to her, Geraldine lay back and closed her eyes.

She'd vanquished her shadows.

For now.

THE NEIGHBORHOOD HOA

Death started it.

In Robbie Wilson's front yard, rows of upturned earth belched foulness into the air, cloaking the house like a heavy robe. He stood on the porch with his stomach churning, clutching a shovel. In his other dirt-covered fist, he held a letter. With a grimace, he looked across to the beings on the other side of his fence.

The Homeowners Association board members stood on the sidewalk, drooling and gnashing their teeth like timbers beneath a saw blade. Their mouths twisted, jaws cracked, and black oozing sores popped with pus. They drooled in ravenous hunger, as if all they'd eaten was tainted meat and sour milk, eyes sunken and hollow, skin like week-old meat left out in the sun. They demanded he repair the yard and threatened more fines.

The other neighbors couldn't take it anymore, fearing for their children, exhausted by the nit-picking. One threw water balloons filled with cat food and anchovies at them. Another took a shit on each of their lawns. Another didn't give a fuck anymore—he took a flamethrower to his own house. The house burned down, each lick of flame a victory and the smoke a roast of chicken.

"I'm waiting!" Robbie pointed at the graves. "Only a matter of time."

Growls escalated. He spied the lush, manicured neighborhood beyond the HOA board members. He couldn't say his HOA wasn't diligent. They banged on the fence's gate, attempting to turn the intricate handle with decomposing fingers.

"Oh, no, you don't. You'll not get me for having my grass too high!" Robbie pointed again at the furrowed rows. "They're coming! Wait!"

He'd show Death who was boss. No more unexpected snatches of his family. Carting off his loved ones in the uncertainty of night or wrapped in the rough blanket of illness. He'd consulted the stars, the witches, the woods and now he had done it.

The HOA had been known to force compliance by murdering the residents, all but one. The sole, living person bore the heavy weight of fulfilling the HOA requirements. Alone. Grieving. Aching both physically and mentally, and beneath the crushing task, the lingering HOA board members, looming and gnashing their teeth, waiting for him to make mistake.

Robbie stood on the porch and listened.

Watched.

Waited.

The trees rustled, shadows danced.

The zombies moaned like little girls watching "Nosferatu" for the twelfth time.

"Patience!" He gestured with the shovel to the lawn.

After a few more minutes, his grip slipped.

Robbie balled up the HOA letter and threw it.

It made a perfect arc in the air, a swooshing whoosh as it landed on the last step.

The zombies roared.

They howled at the litter.

"Sorry!" Robbie shouted. He bit his lip. "Come on."

Then, as if hearing him, a mound of dirt rose like a tumor. It spread in waves over the lush grass, pulsing and undulating like a giant beating heart—a big bloated belly filled with putrid pond water. A hand broke through the earth with an accompanying moan. Muffled, but somehow a harmonious chorus, the others broke open. Robbie shrieked as adrenaline and joy rushed through him.

"YES!" He hurried down the steps.

He reached the first grave, closest to the house. With his heart hammering, he grabbed his wife Margo's hand and helped hoist her from the burial bed. The irony of how he'd helped hoist her into their carriage on their wedding day wasn't lost on him.

She sat up, covered in earth, with rocks, worms, and insects clinging to her short afro and along her eyebrows. With a mouth still attached, she growled in hunger. Robbie patted her shoulder, careful to keep his hands out of range, and hurried over to the other family members.

The kids, being full of youthful vigor, had clamored to free themselves and even now, wandered around the yard, stumbling along the cut, immaculate grass surrounding the graves.

"See! There!" Robbie said to the HOA board members. "I did it. I DID it!"

The HOA mob became quiet. Oozing eyeballs and drooling mouths watched Robbie's family make their way up the flat steps into what remained of the house, trails of dirt and debris following behind them like tails. With a singular groan, the HOA mob shuffled off down the sidewalk, away from the house, away from the gate, away from Robbie.

Robbie lowered his arm and sighed. "I told them I'd do it. I just needed time."

He picked up the HOA warning letter, unballed it, and read it again.

"You are in violation of our rebirth regulation. The majority of your house must be reborn. You have until October 31st to comply. Sincerely, The Neighborhood Homeowners Association."

THE GAME

"Come away from the screen door, Akilah." Grandmama clasped her hand on Akilah's slender shoulder and guided her away from the storm door. "Ain't you playin' this game here with granddad?"

"But, it's sunny outside." Akilah pouted, her full lower lip extended in sadness. She plopped down on the couch, feeling the plastic protectant complain as she did so. The basketball rested in her lap.

"It's also raining," Granddaddy Harold said from his recliner.

Akilah put the ball to the side, hopped down, and crawled onto his recliner's arm. "How does the sky do that?"

"Do what?" he asked, looking around her to see the old spaghetti western .

"Like, how is it rainy and be sunny too?"

"Ah, well, the Devil is beating his wife," Granddaddy Harold said.

"Harold!" Grandmama rebuked from the upstairs hall-way. "She's only 7!"

"I'm mature for my age! Everybody says so!" Akilah shouted back. Then she smiled. "Why does the Devil beat his wife? How the devil get a wife? Isn't he bad?"

Granddaddy Harold paused his western and turned to his precocious granddaughter. He took a breath, and said, "There's a lid for every pot and most everyone deserves love. People aren't all bad or all good, Kee Kee, but it's what we decide to do that's good and bad."

Akilah giggled at his use of her nickname.

"Momma said the Devil is evil."

"He is now, but he used to be an angel, remember? He decided to do something horrible," Granddaddy explained. "That's why he's in hell. He's still being punished."

Akilah's mouth made a round *O* of astonishment. She fingered one of her braids. "Granddaddy, why does he beat his wife? That's mean."

Granddaddy Harold scratched his silver afro. "Well, he doesn't hurt her physically, but he's beating her in a game they're playing."

Akilah's face wrinkled. "A game? The Devil plays a game?"

"Oh yes. Don't you like playing games?" He tickled her a bit, and she squealed in delight.

"Yeah!"

"You're going to make her have an asthma attack! Harold!" Grandmomma shouted down the stairs.

Granddaddy Harold paused his tickle assault and waited for Akilah to catch her breath. He picked up the remote. Maybe the laughter would get his attention.

She wrapped her arms around his neck, fidgeting at his beard when it brushed her arm. "What game do they play?"

"Oh, they play lots of games, but mostly cards," Granddaddy Harold said.

"Why is it raining and sunny?"

"Well, you see, when the Devil is winning, the sun shines as when he was the Angel of Light. His wife is losing, so she cries, and that is the rain you see. If it gets stormy and thunders or lightning crashes, then they're neck and neck, battling out to see who wins. You don't see the sun then because it's such a tight game."

"Oh, that's weird." Akilah climbed down from the recliner and back onto the couch, cradling her basketball. "So, when it's sunny, the Devil is winning?"

"Shush, Kee Kee. Just like you, they don't play games all the time. When the sun is shining, the sun's just shining."

Grandmomma's house shoes slapped on the steps as she made her way back downstairs. She put her hands on her hips and *tsked* at her husband.

"You didn't need to tell her that story, Harold."

He glanced back over his shoulder. "No, but she enjoyed it. Anyway, you should've let me win. Then she could've gone out and played."

DARK AUGUST RAIN

Agnes Gray clutched her oak bookshelf for strength. She knew a killer, a good, efficient murderer. He swarmed upon the unsuspecting victim and—without mercy—pounced. With thick, ruddy hands, the brightness of their life left in horrible gasps and frantic clawing, desperate to remain. In its wake, blue faced, eyes bulging and dotted with petechiae hemorrhaging, the woman—it was always a woman—met her tragic end.

And Agnes had witnessed every single one of his crimes.

She had, in fact, known him almost her entire life.

Because, well, she had *created* the bastard.

Kent Mulberry's latest dark deeds lay sprawled across the hardwood floor on white, 8x11 sheets. Stained with black printer ink and Agnes's sweat, the remnants of his misdeeds frolicked with dust bunnies and cat hair. At a clap of thunder, she jumped. Heart hammering, she let go of the shelf and the breath she was holding.

"It's done," she whispered and turned to face him.

"It is," Came the response, echoing through the study. The cold air that slipped down between the fabric of her sweater and her cotton blouse gave her a chill. Agnes offered her best grin, wide with a pinch of flirtation, to disarm Kent's disappointment.

Several short feet away, Kent Mulberry, he of her imagination, gave her the usual joyless smirk. Dressed in his customary charcoal gray three-piece suit and ebony wingtips, he placed his hands in his pockets while striking the pose commonly found on her book covers.

"I'm a shadow of my former shadow," he announced.

"The fans still adore you," Agnes crooned and brush a hand over her outfit. She always felt so inadequate around him, underdressed next to his flawless English outfit.

"We only ever meet over a dead body." Kent grimaced and then sighed.

"This is our last, and you've made it good."

Kent quirked an eyebrow but did not reply. She liked that about him. Silent. Strong. Dangerous. He'd made her wealthy, popular, and adored. Despite that truth, she needed to move on to other projects.

"You in here?" questioned a lyrical voice from the doorway.

Agnes shooed Kent out of her writing office. He vanished in a smoky swirl that smelled of expensive cologne. Just in time for Sasha Thorne to poke her head in. Long, wavy braids spilled down to her shoulders. Square, black-rimmed glasses on her face made her appear smart and savvy. She smiled when she saw Agnes and came into the study.

"Evening Sasha." Agnes glanced behind her to make sure Kent had left before putting her full attention back on the literary agent.

The literary agent and lover of all Kent Mulberry stories had come down from Chicago to Knoxville, to usher in the close of the series persona. Sasha discovered Agnes Gray's little anti-hero nearly a decade ago and had helped bring

Kent Mulberry to life. Like some literature godmother, Sasha had been the architect of making Agnes's writing dreams come true, so it was fitting she'd come to see the series end.

Despite being middle-aged, Sasha was all lush curves and perfection. Her flawless looks could've been airbrushed if she wasn't standing in front of Agnes. Smooth, dark skin, bee-stung lips, and bright, intelligent eyes set in a heart-shaped face. Sasha's outward beauty took a backseat to the woman's cunning and her ability to sell her clients' manuscripts, though. They weren't friends, but Agnes respected her.

"I thought you were talking to someone in here." Sasha came all the way inside, searching the room as she did so.

Agnes blanched. "Um, no, just brainstorming out loud. So, let's get ready to go."

Sasha shook her head. "Not so fast, Aggie. I want to see it."

Agnes froze. Sasha always wanted to see *it*. "Now?"

Sasha nodded. "It's done, right?"

Sighing, Agnes squatted down and began to collect the sheets from the floor.

"Right?"

"Yes. We finished it only a few minutes ago."

Sasha laughed. "Love how you talk about Kent like he's alive."

Agnes forced a grin. "Writers' characters *are* alive."

"I'm going to have to take your word for it." Sasha bent down to help collect the papers.

"Don't step on the rug!" Agnes flung out her hand to stop Sasha from stepping forward.

Sasha swallowed audibly and cleared her throat. "Those

are some strange markings on that area rug. It's not Oriental."

"No, uh, it isn't an Oriental rug, nor Persian…"

The rug… Agnes glanced down at its dark markings, and then quickly away, unable to complete the thought. Agnes's mouth had gone dry. With trembling hands, she shuffled up the papers with those stacked on her desk. That was close.

"Well, Indian then?" Sasha bent down to look closer at the rug, but she didn't try to touch it again.

A deep rumbling of cackles erupted as the lights flickered. The thunder rumbled so violently, the walls seemed to shake.

Kent.

His voice roared all around her. *Foolish woman! The rug's not Indian. She's supposed to be the smart one?*

"Hush up!" Agnes whispered.

Sasha froze. "Pardon?"

The sooner they left, the better. Kent didn't like visitors, and despite how much Sasha's assistance had helped Agnes's career, he didn't like Sasha. So she hurried to the study door, grabbing her purse in the process. She waved to Sasha frantically.

"Let's go. I think there's a break in the storm." Agnes forced her voice to be calm.

Sasha straightened. "Are you all right? What about the book?"

"Yes. Right as rain." Agnes forced a smile she didn't feel. "If we don't go now, we're going to be late. The book will be here when we get back."

Sasha hesitated and then walked over to give her a one-armed hug. "This new book is going to blast right up to the top. I can feel it."

Agnes swallowed the hard lump of emotion in her throat. "Yes. Me too."

They left the study and walked to the door. Agnes paused to pull on her rainslicker and boots while Sasha tightened the belt of her trench coat and picked up her umbrella. Agnes knew Kent was watching, listening.

"Don't you get lonely in this big, empty house?"

Agnes hadn't ever been alone. Kent had always been there. "No. Not at all."

Overhead the rumbling continued. It sounded like Kent's grumbling when displeased. She shuddered and hunched deeper into her coat. She never liked Kent when displeased. His tantrums never ended well.

THE ANGER BURNED INSIDE. QUIETER NOW, BUT still riotous in its fury, it beat in fast pumps through him. He longed to punch that Sasha right in the center of her self-righteous smugness. The respect for his creator, his *birth mother*, stayed his hand, but the itch kept insisting. His hands became tight fists, one around his cane, the other around the cool office air. She'd nearly stepped on him with her expensive Jimmy Choos. The *nerve*.

Outside, the storm raged in concert with his fury.

Maybe it had everything to do with the hypocrisy that remained a constant and consistent button of annoyance. Yet, to pretend that Kent didn't exist was to invite denial. To deny to oneself is to court insanity. He wouldn't tempt that darkness, nor should Agnes. They'd been together for a long time.

So, Kent's fury fed his growing dislike for Agnes's so-called attempts to banish him from existence. In the past, he'd managed to talk her into keeping him, telling her to think of the fans, those dedicated readers who bombarded her social media with protests. She'd agreed. But now Sasha had talked her into ending him for good. Of course, he protested, cajoled, and even, dare he say it—begged.

The End had been a great source of accomplishment for him, but now that it would be his final ending, Kent felt the need to sever their partnership, too. Agnes's veiled strokes to what she believed was his fragile ego had done nothing for him, except breed *contempt* for her. As if he needed public appreciation to feel whole. Kent breathed. Perhaps he did. She manipulated the other characters like all were action figures just so she would be lifted up—praised and acknowledged. Agnes Gray, great mystery writer. But readers clamored for *his* retention *for* him.

And it was time he struck out on his own.

As the rain drummed out his thoughts, Kent swirled above the carpet, an angry cloud readying to rain on Agnes's parade.

"THIS IS A DARK AUGUST." AGNES PLACED THE cloth napkin across her lap.

The heavy summer squall seemed less threatening now that she'd left the house. Seated at the Writers of Mystery Awards banquet, Agnes finally relaxed. Kent had settled down or gone to sleep. The ending of his books hit him hard.

"Why?" Sasha fingered the restaurant's attempt at silverware with an amused look on her face. When she glanced up to meet Agnes's eyes, she asked, "What makes it dark?"

Agnes shifted uncomfortably as others at the table turned to face her. With a deep, steadying breath, she told her fellow diners and writers seated near her the truth. They leaned in, their curiosity ignited by Sasha's frankness.

"In this area, the rains come in August, every August. A monsoon type of rain. Every day. It rains so much, the skies are black, dark. Hence, a dark August. But the darkness isn't just in the absence of sunlight, but also in the vile and evil acts people perform as a result." Agnes reached for her water glass and sipped.

Sasha was seated to her right and tugged on her sleeve. Out of the corner of her mouth, Sasha remarked, "Really! Good hook for the new book."

"There's an ache to the evening when the rains come, as if the swollen sky's burden had become too great." Agnes fingered the fork.

"Are you all right?" Sasha whispered. She leaned over to Agnes and touched her hand.

Agnes opened her mouth to speak, but a thin pain filtered into her forehead. Kent's voice spoke, clear and loud, his tone undeniable—rage. *Silence! Stop rambling on like some lost hippie high on medical marijuana. Is this the future you have so quickly embraced?*

Each word was an ice pick slash through her mind, as if he meant to punch her until she did indeed become silent—perhaps permanently. She winced, her eyes shutting to the agony. When Kent got angry, he knew just how to make her pay for his fury.

"Yes. Yes!" Agnes whispered through the pain. *Stop Kent! Stop!* She clutched her napkin, twisting in her hands to keep from screaming outright.

When she opened her eyes, she saw Sasha sitting back in her chair with an expression of concern and horror. Her hand remained extended toward her but didn't touch her. Just like in the study, Sasha seemed frozen with indecision.

"Aggie? Aggie!" Sasha inched up in her chair.

"I'm fine. It's just a headache." Agnes forced a smile and nodded at the others at the table, all glaring at her with a mixture of concern and amusement. "Must be the wine."

Sasha frowned but didn't contradict her.

"Then hold off on the champagne. Mixing them will only compound your headache," another writer chimed in.

The others murmured agreements, and to Agness' relief, turned their attention to the speaker.

Except Sasha.

Always watching with a shrewdness that Agnes usually enjoyed, Sasha folded her arms in her lap. Agnes pushed her fear and the rippling pain from Kent's mental assault aside. There wasn't any doubt that Sasha had seen enough to be suspicious. Agnes took solace in the notion that she and Kent Mulberry would be no more after tonight.

Once the manuscript went to Chicago with Sasha, she'd take that rug outside and burn it. When the rain stopped, as soon as the squall ceased.

"Thank you for coming down here and for accompanying me to the banquet." Agnes climbed into the driver's side of the car with fear creeping up her neck.

Sasha got in on the passenger side, her clutch in her hand. "Oh, no you don't. I left my rental at your place, and you're not getting out of handing over that manuscript so I can read it on the plane."

"I can drop it off tomorrow morning, before breakfast." She gripped the steering wheel and tried to come up with rebuttals to Sasha's claims. Normally, she let her come in and the two would spend hours in the study or out on the patio enjoying a bottle of wine, with cheese and crackers or cake, as Sasha talked royalties, rights, and promotions.

"And the rental?" Sasha shook her head and giggled.

"I will return it to the rental car company after I drop you off at the airport." Agnes felt the first beads of sweat appear on her brow. She wanted to run, to shove Sasha out of the car if only to keep her safe.

Safe? From what? Nothing had occurred to indicate Sasha had been in any danger back at the house, but Agnes had a sick feeling in the pit of her stomach. As the rain drummed down on the car's roof, Agnes felt like it beat out a warning across her back.

"That's nonsense! I'm going to that big, dark house of yours and getting my hands on your latest masterpiece. What's wrong with you, anyway?" Sasha buckled her seatbelt. "You've been acting strange all night. Coming out of nowhere with all that talk about a dark August."

Agnes struggled to keep from lashing out at the literary agent, from screaming that she should run out into the falling rain. Although it sounded preposterous on its face,

Agnes couldn't explain why she felt the pressure of fear fondling her emotional strings, but she did.

"Listen, Sasha…"

"No, don't tell me. You don't have to explain," Sasha said with her finger to Agnes's lips. "I know the idea to end the Kent Mulberry series was mine, and I know I sort of strong-armed you into it. It still must be hard to do it."

Agnes removed Sasha's hand with a squeeze. "I agreed to do it. It was time. It's just, well, there's a lot going on. Kent had been my security blanket, and now, well, that's over. I'm already thinking about a new character and series."

Sasha relaxed. "Great. Then let me pick up Kent and take him on back to Chi-town."

Agnes nodded and started the car. With her heart in her throat, she gave Sasha what she thought was a reassuring nod and pointed the car in the direction of home. Perhaps she could fish it out of the study and get it back to Sasha before the woman came into the house. Yes. She didn't want Sasha in the house.

The drive home took her along darkened streets shiny from the rain, punctuated by claps of thunder and flashes of lightning. Sasha drifted off to sleep, but the closer Agnes came to her home, the heavier the pit in her stomach became.

All too soon, she pulled into the garage. The downpour continued uninterrupted and with complete indifference. The overhead light flickered as if winking at their arrival. Agnes swallowed and got out slowly. Sasha already had escaped the car and was fishing around in her purse.

"I know I put the car keys in here," Sasha mumbled.

"Stay here and I'll go get the manuscript." Agnes hurried

to the door, unlocked it, and entered her house before Sasha could reply.

Already, the pressure folded on her the closer she came to the study. Kent. Once she switched on the study's light, the rug's unique patterns illuminated. Black wingtips materialized dead center in the rug's oval markings. Slowly, Kent arrived until the top of his head finished appearing, and he breathed. He put those angry gray eyes on Agnes and she came to a halt. He flexed his body as he filled in from Agnes's imagination.

As he'd done for the last ten years. Thunder rumbled overhead as if announcing his arrival.

"Good evening." Kent bowed briefly before righting himself.

Agnes nodded, but headed over to her desk. She collected the papers to her chest and then secured them quickly with a rubber band. She kept her back to Kent and avoided stepping on the rug itself.

"What are you doing, Aggie?" Kent asked, and despite the question, his voice held all hints of amusement.

She didn't answer him as she turned to walk out of the study. Just as she looked up, the thunder roared and as it tapered off, a panic-stricken cry rose.

"Who?" Sasha questioned from the doorway. Her face looked like she'd been sucking on a lemon, her cell phone clutched in one hand, her purse in the other. Her eyes were the size of saucers.

"I'm Kent Mulberry, and I'm tired of hiding from you, you pathetic woman. "

Agnes *squeed* on reflex, before she pursed her lips with distaste. She went to stand beside Sasha. "Kent!"

"You're real?" Sasha stumbled backward.

"Not only am I real, I'm fear itself." Kent stepped toward them, a broad grin across his face.

"No! Sasha, Kent's a piece of my imagination." Agnes reached for her, but Sasha recoiled.

With brooding interest, Kent jerked his head around as lightning rippled through the darkness outside. "A piece of your imagination? People enjoy violence and death as long as they can't really smell the blood and bile and hear the wretched screams. From the distance of their sofa safety, I give them that rush of Neanderthal that resides buried in their DNA. I pacify their fear and they love it!"

Agnes could hardly believe it. For as long as she could remember, Kent had remained anchored in her imagination, but now she watched in absolute terror as he stepped off the rug and headed directly for them.

"Stop it!" Agnes launched herself in front of Sasha only a fraction of a second before Kent leapt at her, his hands outstretched toward the agent's throat. Both of them tumbled to the floor. She thought to banish him with the mere thought of telling him to go home, but even as she did this, Kent remained.

He wouldn't leave.

Kent sniggered and stepped back from them. Agnes's heart galloped in her chest at the sound. Agnes thought of all the women Kent had murdered in the novels she wrote.

"Trying to banish me, Aggie? I hear you, in here." He tapped his temple with a gloved finger, and he still wore a big, cold grin. "It isn't working."

No, it wasn't, but that didn't stop him from enjoying it. His joy and absolute lack of a moral compass were the traits that readers loved about him. Modern readers enjoyed the fact that Kent remained true to himself, and honest about his intentions and thirst for bloodshed. Kent Mulberry's "Berries" blared about him in memes, fanfiction, and merchandizing.

"Get out of my way, Aggie," Kent said calmly.

The roaring of the storm outside fell to a hushed shower. Behind her, Agnes heard Sasha struggle to stand as she grunted and huffed out her strain.

Agnes turned to Sasha and shoved the manuscript into her hands. "Take this!"

Sasha took it with confusion marring her features. Agnes grabbed Sasha by the shoulders, spun her around, and pushed her toward the door. "RUN!"

"No!" Kent shoved Agnes out of his way.

Stunned, Sasha gaped at Kent before her fight-or-flight instinct kicked in. Kent punched her, but unlike the characters in Agnes' novels, Sasha, who hailed from the south side of Chicago, didn't fall like a sack of potatoes. She took the hit like she'd been hit before. Clutching the manuscript to her chest, Sasha seemed to wake up.

"Aggie, run! Come on!" Sasha screamed as she kicked off her shoes.

Agnes got to her feet and watched as Kent swung at Sasha again. The literary agent avoided his punch, but only just. No longer a phantom, Kent learned how to manipulate his body faster and faster as he manifested into flesh. Soon, he'd get the hang of it, and then, he'd be just as deadly in real life as he was on the page.

"Run! Just go! I'm fine!" Agnes picked up the Navajo vase on her desk and smashed it over Kent's head. It didn't break as cleanly as they did in the movies, and it didn't stop him. It made him pause, though, and as he did, Sasha scrambled out of the study.

He turned on Agnes and pushed her; she fell back against her desk. Kent's cold gray eyes looked like the angry storm clouds outside as they hovered over her. His mouth a slash, his gloved hands now fists, he growled. Agnes didn't try to run. She heard the interior door slam and the garage door open.

Sasha had escaped! The manuscript would live on.

"I'm going to kill you for that. We've never let one escape. Never!" Kent closed the short distance between them, a fast-approaching force.

"No, we never have." Agnes swallowed and conjured a calm she hadn't felt until she heard Sasha's car leaving.

He grinned, and Agnes met his gaze with a smile of her own. She wouldn't scream or close her eyes like the female victims she wrote about—because she wasn't one of those. Not a victim. A *sacrifice*. She walked willingly into the storm that was Kent Mulberry with her eyes wide open.

Kent's grin faltered. Her behavior disturbed him, no doubt.

He stroked her cheek with a gloved hand. "It's rare for one to kill their god."

Before she could reply, Kent grabbed her throat with both hands, and squeezed, but just as fast, a shriek of pain erupted from him as he staggered back from her, releasing her throat. Gasping for air, Agnes dropped onto her desk, the bloodied letter opener in her hand. She'd grabbed it just seconds earlier, keeping it hidden in her slicker's long sleeves.

"What have you done? It hurts!" Kent roared as the rain

faded in its intensity. He clamored at his shirt. The inky spot blossomed as he backed up onto the rug in the center of the floor.

"What I've always done. Banished you!" Agnes croaked, rubbing her throat.

"Why? Why would you? I *made* you!" Kent looked at the blood on his hands with a strange mix of confusion and fascination. It had a dark, nearly black color, like ink.

"You didn't make me, but I will end you." She moved around her desk, dug in the top drawer, and pulled out her matches. Aromatherapy helped shepherd her through writer's block, so she kept matches on hand for her candles. She scurried over to the rug, and as Kent collapsed to his knees squealing about his injury, she lit a match and tossed it onto the rug. The flames caught and soon burned.

Kent screamed. He howled with agony and Agnes clapped her hands over her ears. Her creation, her invention, dissolved into nothing but a puddle of water and what looked like ink. It pooled where Kent had been, and the rug was rendered to cinders, leaving only burnt stains.

Outside, the clouds parted, and the moon came into view.

A dark August no more.

SOUTHERN GOTHIC THEMES

The following are common themes in Southern Gothic literature, here with the stories in which they are featured most heavily:

Alienation

- Dogwood Stories
- As Dark the Night
- Sunshine

Decay and Dilapidated Settings

- The Guardian
- The Game
- Neighborhood HOA
- Dark August Rain

Poverty

- Sweet Tooth
- Turn of a Leaf

Exploring Madness

- The Tell-Tale Tattoo
- Lipstick Smile
- Shepherds of the Storm

BOOK CLUB DISCUSSION QUESTIONS

1. In which stories do you note the most classically gothic tropes? How are they put to use in contemporary cities and other modern settings?

2. Here we meet many young protagonists who are swept along by forces they cannot control—prejudiced societies, generational poverty, disembodied evils. Which of these characters did you feel the most sympathy for, and why?

3. Several of the stories in this collection involve people taking back their power from nefarious entities and skewed systems. Which of these was most satisfying, and why do you think so?

4. Strong bonds—familial, romantic, platonic— exist between the characters who populate these stories. How did these bonds help the characters persevere through challenges? How did they make the characters act rashly or put themselves at risk?

5. The idea of madness is frightening in part because it involves a loss of control. In which of these stories does madness seem most dangerous? Is there any solace to be found in madness for any of these characters?

6. How does urban decay and dilapidation reflect a society's historical traumas and generational violence? In which of these stories do you see those parallels clearly, and in what ways?

BIBLIOGRAPHY

Bjerre, Thomas Ærvold. 8 June 2017. https://doi.org/10.1093/acrefore/
9780190201098.013.304

ABOUT THE AUTHOR

Nicole Givens Kurtz has been called "a genre polymath who does crime, horror, and Science Fiction and Fantasy (Book Riot)." Her horror weird western, Sisters of the Wild Sage was included in Book Riot's "The Best of the West: 8 Alternative History Westerns."

She's a two-time Atomacon Palmetto Scribe Award winner (2021 and 2022), a recipient of the Ladies in Horror Grant, and a recipient of the HWA Diversity Grant. With over 20 years in publishing, Nicole has over 50 published short stories and is the editor of groundbreaking anthologies, *SLAY: Stories of the Vampire Noire* and *Blackened Roots: An Anthology of the Undead* with Tonia Ransom.

www.nicolegivenskurtz.net

instagram.com/Nicolegkurtz

facebook.com/nicolegkurtz

amazon.com/stores/Nicole-Givens-Kurtz/author/B0057X-EF0G

bsky.app/profile/nicolegkurtz.bsky.social

If you are a fan of horror stories and tales, you'll want to follow Undertaker Books.
We're bringing you stories to take to your grave.